Once Upon A Dream

Verses Of Twilight

Edited By Lynsey Evans

First published in Great Britain in 2024 by:

Young Writers Est. 1991

Young Writers
Remus House
Coltsfoot Drive
Peterborough
PE2 9BF
Telephone: 01733 890066
Website: www.youngwriters.co.uk

All Rights Reserved
Book Design by Ashley Janson
© Copyright Contributors 2024
Softback ISBN 978-1-83565-466-8
Printed and bound in the UK by BookPrintingUK
Website: www.bookprintinguk.com
YB0591M

FOREWORD

Welcome Reader, to a world of dreams.

For Young Writers' latest competition, we asked our writers to dig deep into their imagination and create a poem that paints a picture of what they dream of, whether it's a make-believe world full of wonder or their aspirations for the future.

The result is this collection of fantastic poetic verse that covers a whole host of different topics. Let your mind fly away with the fairies to explore the sweet joy of candy lands, join in with a game of fantasy football, or you may even catch a glimpse of a unicorn or another mythical creature. Beware though, because even dreamland has dark corners, so you may turn a page and walk into a nightmare!

Whereas the majority of our writers chose to stick to a free verse style, others gave themselves the challenge of other techniques such as acrostics and rhyming couplets.

Each piece in this collection shows the writers' dedication and imagination – we truly believe that seeing their work in print gives them a well-deserved boost of pride, and inspires them to keep writing, so we hope to see more of their work in the future!

CONTENTS

Alkrington Primary School, Middleton

James Smith (9)	1
Carabelle Quansah (9)	2
Oliver Howard (8)	4
Bella Michaels (8)	5
Eva Swindles (9)	6
Sola Fadahunsi (8)	7
Holly Turner (9)	8
Evie McGuire (8)	9
Noah McCullagh (8)	10
Raiah Fishwick (8)	11

Boltons CE Primary School, Wigton

Quinlan Ion (9)	12
Lottie Prescott (8)	13
Nicole Todd (8)	14
Laurence Merrick (8)	15
Jacob Hunter (8)	16
Ailsa Todd (9)	17
Mack Jourdain (7)	18
Carys Williams (9)	19
Josie Cornthwaite (8)	20
Aleasha Johnston (8)	21
Ross Creighton (8)	22
Brogan Airey (8)	23

Crianlarich Primary School, Crianlarich

Erin Kyle (11)	24
Penny Murdoch-Lindsay (10)	26
Samvrita Santhosh	27

Callum Kyle (9)	28
Mia Narog (9)	29
Hunter Frost (9)	30
Evey Lings (9)	31
Charlie Murdoch-Lindsay (10)	32
Ben MacLennan (9)	33
Kevin Nemeth (10)	34

Dell Primary School, Oulton Broad

Tahlia-Rose Clarke (7)	35
Louie Irving (8)	36
Isaac Collyer (8)	37
Isla Albery (8)	38
Bobby Borrett (8)	39
Lucie Howard (8)	40
Honor Newrick Thorpe (9)	41
Florence Minney (8)	42
Jack Purser (8)	43
Saxon Turner (9)	44
Molly Jones (9)	45
Alfie Doughty (7)	46
Lucy Norman (8)	47
Meta Marcinkeviciute (9)	48
Thea Wills (9)	49
Alfie Cutler (9)	50
Millie Savannah Rose Cook (8)	51
Rocco Dyke (8)	52
Esther Durrant (8)	53
Kelsey Cook (8)	54
Ruby-Mai Curtis (9)	55
Ethan Zhang (8)	56
Isla Day (7)	57
Ellie Folasade Davies (7)	58
Katie Everett (7)	59

Ewan Watson (9)	60
Roxy Harrod (8)	61
Darcie Tonks (9)	62
Matthew Hathaway (8)	63
Harrison Maher (8)	64
Indiana Marjoram (8)	65
Millie-Rose Bowman (9)	66
Lillie Cornwell (8)	67
Eva Hart (9)	68
Harry Youngs (8)	69
Sienna Whiteland (8)	70
Florence Vincent (9)	71
Scarlett Humphreys (9)	72
Arlo Hender (8)	73
Henley Wills (9)	74
Oscar Edmunds (8)	75
Lenny Cole (9)	76
William Copping (7)	77
Zaccai Sule (9)	78
Emilly Hammond (8)	79
Jasmine Dean (8)	80
Ronan Langdale (8)	81
Brooklyn Withers (8)	82
Charlotte King (8)	83

Flakefleet Primary School, Fleetwood

Amelie Holden (11)	84
Brody Wilson (10)	86
Freddie William Butterfield (10)	87
Ralph Broadbent (10)	88
Ellouise-Mai Wright (10)	89
Miley-Rae Birch (11)	90
Megan Crane (11)	91
Aniyah Stokes (11)	92
Kacie Brooke (11)	93
Velvet Cunningham (11)	94
Brooke Nullall (10)	95
Jenson Jessop (11)	96
Jasmine Gardener (11)	97

Goldbeaters Primary School, Edgware

Danish Mohammed Ali (10)	98
Salma Farah (11)	99
Zainab Dahir (10)	100
Elisa Sheikhi (11)	101

Laurieston Primary School, Laurieston

Harper Duncan (9)	102
Oscar McRobbie (9)	104
Arran Blue (9)	105
Jamie Smith (9)	106
Alexander Vasilev (9)	107
Benjamin Mackintosh (9)	108
Eli Paterson (9)	109
Matthew Darrell (9)	110
Emily Meiklejohn (9)	111
Charlotte Dewar (9)	112
Freya Sturrock (9)	113
Leo McArthur (9)	114
Summer Begg (9)	115
Laila Stewart (9)	116

Perry Court E-ACT Academy, Hengrove

Kaddy Nyanfora (8)	117
Zara Davey (8)	118
Sophie Stratford (8)	120
Laya Alznati (10)	121
Louie Phillips (7)	122
Tara Nasiri Khanghahi (9)	123
Summerlee Filer (9)	124
Mariana Vicentim (8)	125
Pritanshi Gundemoni (6)	126
Brihati Gundemoni (7)	127
Maddison-Leigh Pearce (10)	128
Layla Stuckes (10)	129
Yasmina-Roberta Suciachi (10)	130
Josie Gill (7)	131
Scarlet Smart (9)	132

Beau Chapman (10)	133
Disini Pallwela (7)	134
Chanade Sheridan (10)	135
Freya Topp (11)	136
Freya Borsay (9)	137
L M Dinugi (10)	138
Mollie Parker (11)	139
Hazel Autumn Lewin Gilbert (8)	140

Regis Manor Primary School, Milton Regis

James Clarck (9)	141
John Olamiko (9)	142
Edmile Valantinaviciute (9)	143
Teegan Charles (11)	144
Josette Kusi (9)	146
Alexandra Ciurca (10)	147
Christabella Akiri (10)	148
Ellie Sheridan (9)	149
Amelia Maitland (9)	150

Ruskin Academy, Wellingborough

Hollie Knight (11)	151
Charlie Stronach (8)	152
Oliwia Dziecielska (10)	153
Patricia Zdrinca (10)	154
Holly Maginnis (10)	155
Oceana Munton (10)	156
Maia Rickett-Browne (10)	157
Leon Bailey (10)	158

Springbank Academy, Eastwood

Grace Harvey (8)	159
TJ Smith (8)	160
Lucas Fowers (8)	161
Kai Hayes (9)	162
Oscar Woodcock (9)	163
Layla Hicking (8)	164
L Elizabeth North (8)	165
Laila-Mai Catchpole (8)	166
Lilly Daykin (9)	167

Charlie Needham (9)	168
Maddie Watson (8)	169
Emmie Belcher (9)	170
James Vincett (9)	171
Nathan Stanton-Meakin (8)	172

St Thomas Of Canterbury Catholic Primary School, Mitcham

Isabel Potter (10)	173
Gabriela Sacewicz (10)	174
Julia Warian (10)	176
Georgette Nyamekeh (10)	178
Charlotte Nalukobe (11)	179
Zuzanna Ogrodnik (11)	180

Tockington Manor School, Tockington

Kieran Quick (11)	181
Sienna Ricciardi (10)	182
Nitsa Bhadri (11)	183
Harry Preece (10)	184
Sirivaana Vankdoth (10)	186
Isabel Pickavance (11)	187
Amal Lachab (10)	188
Avneet Chohan (11)	190
Ruby Layade (11)	191
George Griffith (10)	192
Albie Palmer (10)	193
Emma Fudulu (10)	194
Stanley Baigent (11)	195
Maximilian Hunt (11)	196
Leon Francken (10)	197
Oliver Galpin (10)	198
Emma Strickland (10)	199
Sophia Heer (11)	200
Joseph Leadbeater (11)	201

Wistow Parochial CofE (VC) School, Wistow

Rhea Mclean (9)	202
Isabella Haddon (10)	203
Annabelle Davis (9)	204
Scarlett Wilson (8)	205
Lorna Wood (9)	206
Georgia Pavey (8)	207
Lydia Jones (10)	208
Florence Ibson (10)	209
Luisa Kehoe (9)	210

THE POEMS

The World Cup

T he best football team, England FC with Fletcher
H i, I'm in Antarctica jumping off a cliff onto the infinite pitch
E xcited but nervous is my feeling, I'm so happy I could reach the ceiling

W e can see people jumping off the cliff, flying onto the infinite pitch
O ff the cliff, into the infinite, where Marcus Rashford passes to Fletcher who crosses to me. I header it back and bicycle kick into the top corner and we win
R eady to celebrate our win
L ook up to the sky and see God saying it's over
D one, it's finally done, we've won!

C oming to score the winning goal is me
U p in the sky is Harry Kane as Jesus
P ut Harry Maguire in our net and he saves all the shots

James Smith (9)
Alkrington Primary School, Middleton

Searching For A Magical Dream

As it says in the title,
All dreams are magical!
Whatever you think of,
And if someone says it is silly,
Just ignore them!
Just be you!

What I'm saying is,
Don't care what others
Think of you!
Even if the president
Said you're ugly or
Something like that,
Defend yourself,
Because you and everyone
Can make dreams come true!

Win or lose, I am
Still going to be happy!
I don't want to be
Like those kids who
Lost and are a crybaby.

I am strong and
Happy and kind
And nice. No one
Likes to feed
Cheese to mice!

Sometimes you have
Nightmares, sometimes
You have dreams!

You should thank God for
It and do what he needs!

Everyone has bad
Decisions, but if you work
Hard and think it
Through like cooking,
You can make something delicious!

Carabelle Quansah (9)
Alkrington Primary School, Middleton

My Pokémon

I'm dreaming
I'm dreaming
I'm dreaming about Pokémon
All through the night
Till morning comes
I'm dreaming

Where is my Pikachu?
Where is my Pikachu?
Is he with my Charizard
Or maybe he's hiding?
Could he be at my night school
Or maybe my house?

I need to find my Pikachu,
Before the battle starts
Can I remember in time?

Oh look, he's hiding in my Poké Ball
Oh Pikachu
Oh Pikachu
Oh how I missed you so.

Oliver Howard (8)
Alkrington Primary School, Middleton

Dream Town

I dream about a world where your imagination comes true.
Last night, I dreamt about it, and I was with you.
We saw fairies, giants, horses and unicorns, every colour you could see.
With a shining sword in a massive stone, which even the strongest giants couldn't free.
We rode dolphins in shiny, sparkling water and clouds like fluffy bees.
I don't feel scared here, as I know I can be me.
I often feel excited about going to bed at night,
With the anticipation of Dream Town filling me with delight.

Bella Michaels (8)
Alkrington Primary School, Middleton

The Cat And The Magic Hat

Last night, I had a dream.
In the dream, there was a cat.
The cat was called Mr Fat.

Mr Fat sat upon a magic mat,
Which made the cat fly like a bat.
On his trip, he saw a rat,
Who said, "You silly pussycat!"
"Come down off that mat,
Before you turn into a splat!"

The cat came down from his mat,
And feasted on the chatty rat.
And that was that.

Eva Swindles (9)
Alkrington Primary School, Middleton

Time Travel

T oday I will time travel,
I n Pompeii,
M y family was there,
E erie explosion.

T raders were trading,
R ound the houses, people were crusading.
A fter the explosion.
V arious catastrophic implosions were in Pompeii,
E ven though we wanted to stay,
L ater that day, we realised we didn't want to die in Pompeii.

Sola Fadahunsi (8)
Alkrington Primary School, Middleton

Olympic Swimmer

S wimming is what I dream about,
W inning is my goal,
I 've trained for the Olympics since I was three,
M y brain is getting more and more focused,
M y head is ringing with excitement,
I 'm gliding through the water,
N ot giving up, even though I'm behind,
G o, go, go, I can see the wall from here.

Holly Turner (9)
Alkrington Primary School, Middleton

My Dream Life

I usually dream of me with ice cream
Jumping into the waterpark.
Splashing my dad with water
Giving me a spark.

Making me laugh,
Making me cry,
Making me go down the waterslide.

Making me smile,
Making me cry,
Making me swim from the crocodile.

Making me happy,
Making me sad,
Making me love the life I have.

Evie McGuire (8)
Alkrington Primary School, Middleton

Life In Hogwarts!

I'm in Hogwarts castle,
It's a bit of a hassle.
I have the best broom,
It goes zoom zoom!
Harry's fighting Voldemort,
He was too young, I thought.
Dumbledore dies,
Draco's spreading lies!

Noah McCullagh (8)
Alkrington Primary School, Middleton

My Dreams

When on the floor, I dance and fly.
I dream of holding the trophies high.
Practice is the key.
Gymnastics is me!

Raiah Fishwick (8)
Alkrington Primary School, Middleton

The Magic Necklace

Once I was a footballer
And the match was tomorrow
So I was about to assemble my
Brand new white, comfy bed.
I placed my mattress,
Well, almost,
Until I found a necklace!
I put it on but it felt odd;
I had no feeling anywhere in my body.
I fell and felt nothing.
Outside, my necklace shot a beam of light,
It broke the lamppost
Creating a trench in the ground.
Terrified, I rushed back to my room
And hid it to cause no more damage.
However, I felt it on my neck the next morning,
And it was a good luck charm.
My match went well
I scored a goal
I was the player of the match.
The trophy was the best goal of all!

Quinlan Ion (9)
Boltons CE Primary School, Wigton

Space

As I was in my upside-down world,
Stepping on my stormy cloud,
Trying to run away because it was too loud,
I wanted to know,
What's down below?
So I hid from the rest,
To find the very best.
I jumped for my life,
It felt like I was in a race,
I was in space!
All the planets looked like my lace.
I fell with a clamber,
As the moon looked like a grey amber,
I was all alone,
All I hoped for was to return home.
I closed my eyes tightly
And grinned delightedly,
I dreamed of waking up back in the comfort of my home.

Lottie Prescott (8)
Boltons CE Primary School, Wigton

Spider In My Room

A spider in my room
In the corner of my wall
When it is time for me to go to bed.
I worried I would not sleep
All night I stared at the creature,
I had to get rid of it somehow.
Should I shout at my dad to come get rid of it?
Should I throw my pillow at it?
They all would not work.
So I got some toilet roll
My heart pounding
My body was shaky
My legs were trembling
My palms were sweaty
At last, I got the courage to stretch up and get it
I threw it out the window
And finally fell asleep.

Nicole Todd (8)
Boltons CE Primary School, Wigton

Rugby

In my dream, I am upset and scared because...
I am seeing bullies, coaches and a humongous pitch.
But suddenly, I saw one of my friends who helped.
Reactively, I wanted to go home,
But my coach told me to play
Because I play in matches so well.
So suddenly, I got the heart to play.
What could stop me now?
Nothing!
I got up and played on.
To be honest, I was impressed.
My parents were impressed as well.
My coach said I'd played so well.
I received the winning trophy.

Laurence Merrick (8)
Boltons CE Primary School, Wigton

Pirates

I was out at sea,
I wondered what I could see.
My ship was fighting a storm,
I woke up at the crack of dawn!
The waves were crashing,
My head was bashing.
There was another ship at sea,
I wondered who it could be.
The clouds were roaring like a lion,
The waves tried to destroy my ship,
They were only trying.
The storm was lashing and making my ship row.
Tiredly on the wave below.
I wondered how far I could go.
I really don't know...

Jacob Hunter (8)
Boltons CE Primary School, Wigton

A Dream Horse

In my dreams, everything at night is magnificent.
Horses before my eyes.
In the forest, my horses glow,
Clippity-clop does she go.

Bright colours blinding my eyes,
As the wind whistle blows with delight.
Her hooves are like gold,
And she is as white as paper.

The only sound you can hear is her swishing tail.
When she jumps and turns, it looks like she's flying,
Like a dolphin jumping out of the water,
Just like a dream horse!

Ailsa Todd (9)
Boltons CE Primary School, Wigton

Archaeologist

Deep in the archaeological mines
A very hard worker was sweating a lot
He'd been mining for so long
His iron pickaxe was about to break
Chipping at the andesite
Suddenly there was a loud bang!
He decided to explore more
As he went further and further
He regretted his choices more and more
Louder and louder it got
And as he turned a corner
He found an ancient Egyptian!

Mack Jourdain (7)
Boltons CE Primary School, Wigton

The Magic Ball

M agic flows across my mind
A nd eventually, I thought that was it!
G ot it! I've got it!
I wonder if it can come to life
C ome to life, it can't come to life

B ut what if it can?
A ll I've dreamed about is this, but what if this is the dream?
L iving life to kick a ball
L iving life to play football.

Carys Williams (9)
Boltons CE Primary School, Wigton

Flying Pegasus

A little speckle in the sky,
High above were pegasus.
Wings so sharp as sharp as a shark bite.

Its body is so white,
As white as a blanket of snow.
Magic so sparkly,
As bright as the sun dancing in its own light.

It flows down, down, down into the real world.
Everybody run away,
There's a pegasus coming this way.

Josie Cornthwaite (8)
Boltons CE Primary School, Wigton

Fairies And Unicorns

As I see the unicorn
Galloping among the trees,
I saw a fairy dancing near the flowers,
I couldn't stop watching them!
The unicorn stopped
It trotted to me
So I got to stroke her.
It made me feel happy.
As the trees swayed in the wind,
Pink leaves flowed gracefully.
I wished upon dreaming,
Of my wonderful dream.

Aleasha Johnston (8)
Boltons CE Primary School, Wigton

A Famous Wizard

My wishes include…
I was begging for a wizard.
For my opportunity to come,
To see the one and only Cristiano Ronaldo.

I wake up at the crack of dawn,
To see the wonder that there could be.

A ticket for me to travel to Spain,
And I only went and met Wayne Rooney on the plane!

Ross Creighton (8)
Boltons CE Primary School, Wigton

A Farmer's Life On A Quad Bike

Zooming along the field on my brand-new quad bike,
Fields as wet as ever,
Ripping up mud and creating tracks,
Travelling as fast as I imagined,
Driving round and round,
Heading back onto the road.

Brogan Airey (8)
Boltons CE Primary School, Wigton

Down In The Mud

I was sitting in the dirt,
With my baby dragon, Squirt,
And my pixie called Charlie,
Was sitting on some barley.

When I saw a coat,
And a miniature boat,
Sticking out the mud,
Then sprung out a plastic pud.

I tried to pick it up,
But it pulled me by a cup,
I got pulled into a mysterious room,
Then I saw a witch's broom.

I was in a witch's cave,
Would I end up like Uncle Dave?
I heard a breath,
Would this be my death?

Turns out she only wanted my pixie,
She needed his bones to give her potion a mixie,
And his blood,
To feed his pet mud.

And for his skin,
I will use it for my gin,
Then I will put his organs in a tin,
And throw the tin in the bin.

The witch did what she said with the pixie,
And gave it a little mixie,
But Squirt started to fly me high,
Turns out I am not going to die.

Erin Kyle (11)
Crianlarich Primary School, Crianlarich

The Monster

Every night I'm stuck on that shore,
As the fog clears, I start to see more,
The water as clear as a crystal,
I see some purple, spiky thistles.

One night when I'm on that shore,
I see too much more,
Two bright eyes shining in the water,
As he comes in, he prepares for his slaughter.

I'm stood there in fear and shock,
But as he emerges, he starts to walk.
An odd, slimy creature,
With non-human features.

He has long, sticky, slimy arms,
Where you will come to harm,
If he gives you a hug,
You turn into a slug.

Then you get eaten by this disgusting thing,
But don't worry because when you wake up,
You will be in your own fantasy land,
Lying in your bed with a new dream of your own.

Penny Murdoch-Lindsay (10)
Crianlarich Primary School, Crianlarich

Just Make A Dream

Once upon a dream,
To be the best me,
But it's not just a dream,
It's the truth sitting upon a tree.
It's not just me fighting for my dreams,
It's everyone, so you see.

They can be famous and fairies,
And dancers and pirates and writers.
Now you see all you can be,
Now, just make a dream.

If you're not sure how to make a dream
It's simple. So you see, here are the rules:
Your dreams have to be as strong as you,
The world is strong, but so are you.
Rule 2: just be you. That's all just 2.
Now close your eyes and make your dream!

Samvrita Santhosh
Crianlarich Primary School, Crianlarich

Why I Love Maths

My name is Callum,
And I like maths,
Sometimes because it makes me laugh,
I love the numbers on the pages,
As they dive right into my brain,
I love maths as it makes my friends laugh,
Now you know why I love maths, so let's have maths every day.

I love the textbook,
It's as red as a rose,
And under light, it really glows,
As the textbook is used by me,
All thanks to the help of the trees,
As they make all the paper out of their wood.

Callum Kyle (9)
Crianlarich Primary School, Crianlarich

Arctic Fox

Beneath the stars of a night sky,
There lies a fox who is quite shy.
Its white coat and black paws,
Shine in the moonlit sky.
I creep up close, taking a look,
There are a million things that the fox has taken.
But its blue eyes suddenly open,
It hisses in fear, and it motions.
It flies and flees and I run after it,
But I suddenly wake up and my light's lit.
And out of the window, what do I see?
An Arctic fox who is about to flee.

Mia Narog (9)
Crianlarich Primary School, Crianlarich

The Fantasy Dream World

The fantasy world, what a wonderful place,
Planes and fame all over the place,
Joyful rides and bikes are full of joy.

No frights or bites and no poison,
Water is crystal clear, no pistols,
Well, there is crystal as big as boulders.

No boulder crushing, also no moulders,
But boulders are the best,
The boulder is the west and best,
When the boulder cracked and smashed,
The boulder was like a mossy tree getting cut.

Hunter Frost (9)
Crianlarich Primary School, Crianlarich

Dinosaur

Dinosaur, dinosaur,
How I hear you roar!
It's loud, it's strong,
Like King Kong,
Dinosaur, dinosaur,
Stamp your feet for me,
Dinosaur, you're silly!
Dinosaur, dinosaur, you are my favourite dino.

Dinosaur, what colour are you?
Your nose is black,
And your body is silver-green,
Teeth are silver,
Eyes red like fire,
And you mean everything to me.

Evey Lings (9)
Crianlarich Primary School, Crianlarich

The Kraken

There once was a Kraken,
Who loved snacking,
On piles of bones,
But one day, he ran out of bones,
He hunted all day.

And all night, yet he
Only had a tiny pile of bones.

He was as purple as an amethyst,
And as big as a mountain,
The next day, he hunted
Again but to no avail, he
Didn't find any fish.

Charlie Murdoch-Lindsay (10)
Crianlarich Primary School, Crianlarich

The Lagoon

There I was sitting at the crystal clear lagoon,
I started to see a creature emerge
With very unusual features
And long slimy tentacles.

His name was Kevin
And he was an eleven,
He liked to eat motorbike bits.

Kevin the Kraken was as slow as a snail,
Then he reached out to me,
But he grabbed a tree.

Ben MacLennan (9)
Crianlarich Primary School, Crianlarich

Dark Forest

A dark forest where there is bark on the trees,
They are tall,
They are also pecked by woodpeckers,
And braces and laces are on the ground,
But a fox jumps out of a small, old house,
The house is abandoned,
Now run from the fox!

Kevin Nemeth (10)
Crianlarich Primary School, Crianlarich

In My Dreams Every Night

In my dreams every night
My dreams every night are filled with delight
Penguins baking yummy cookies
Octopuses are having babies
Sharks are writing amazing stories
While the dolphin shares her worries
The seahorses are playing trumpets
The turtle is under the blanket
A jellyfish is at the park
The whale is in the dark
A shark eel having a spark
The dogfish is sounding a bark
A pufferfish is singing
The clownfish's alarm is ringing
The stingray is playing games
An angelfish is singing names
A squid is skateboarding
The otter is exploring
Maybe I should go to sleep
Instead of trying to do a leap.

Tahlia-Rose Clarke (7)
Dell Primary School, Oulton Broad

In My Dreams Every Night

In my dreams every night,
The moon reflects on the water really bright,
Jellyfish doing frontflips in the deep blue sea,
The octopus boiling a cup of tea,
The big strong turtle playing tennis,
The turtle has long wavy lettuce,
The starfish doing cartwheels on the land,
The sneaky crab walking on the sand,
In the evening the shark gets ready,
In the day a crab eats a cherry,
In the deep blue sea an octopus has a teddy,
The shark is steady and ready,
The jellyfish is in a hurry,
The jellyfish lost his buddy,
The blue whale is playing Uno,
Pufferfish puffering out ready to sumo.

Louie Irving (8)
Dell Primary School, Oulton Broad

In My Dreams Every Night

In my dreams every night
I can see the sun very bright
A shark riding a bike
A fish calling himself Mike
Dolphins diving in the sea
A shark trying to find a key
A blue whale trying to dance
An orca trying to get a glance
Tiger sharks doing the Griddy
All the fish are so pretty
A tiger shark went to Mexico
A fish shouting through a tunnel that echoed
A fish with flames
And a fish playing games
A blobfish driving a tank
A fish pulling pranks
Dolphins fighting in clans
As whales scan
Happy days for fish
All the fish get an itch.

Isaac Collyer (8)
Dell Primary School, Oulton Broad

My Sea Dreams

In my dreams every night
Clownfish orange, fiery bright
Swim in the seas vast and blue
No one likes them but I certainly do
In the depths of the Southern Ocean
I go there with magical potions
The coral sways in the deep sea breeze
It's cool and cold like a deep sea freeze
I like the rainbow turtles' shells
They are as smooth as bright shiny bells
The octopus hides in deep dark holes
While the jellyfish look like they're on poles
Dolphins show up with their cool amazing flips
While the crabs do their cute little snips.

Isla Albery (8)
Dell Primary School, Oulton Broad

In My Dreams Every Night

In my dreams every night,
Stories to tell that could only be cowritten,
Clownfish bowling, getting strikes,
Stingrays posting on Fishbook, getting likes,
Pufferfish going to Mexico,
Sea urchins being stepped on, sending people into pain and inferno,
Electric eel causing pranks,
Bluefish watching outer banks,
Orange fish wagging his tail,
And he's causing trouble,
The snail leaving to juggle,
The shark is surfing and having fun,
The vampire squid winning Uno,
Great white shark using the toilet.

Bobby Borrett (8)
Dell Primary School, Oulton Broad

In My Dreams Every Night

In my dreams every night,
I see fish riding bikes
Clownfish playing tennis
Orcas eating lettuce
Whales in line to fight
While sea snails are being tight
Watch while sea crabs fight
Beluga whales drinking Sprite
A seal at the back line being impolite
Stingrays glide at the side
Dolphins swim with pride
Octopi drive by
While sea horses fix their ties
Sea snails on the trampoline
While sea urchins drink gasoline
While sea snails drive by
You can see orcas in the sky.

Lucie Howard (8)
Dell Primary School, Oulton Broad

In My Dreams

Within my dreams every night,
A lot of jewels all sealed tight.
In the treasure chest that only opens at night,
Every dolphin comes to light.
Whales trying to fit through the gap
But it seems to be too tight.
Then lower down, the octopus enjoys the twilight zone.
An underwater kingdom roams.
Something seems to be stuck tight.
Then a scuba diver swims with delight
Swimming with the whales, there's no commotion
As we all swim in slow motion.

Honor Newrick Thorpe (9)
Dell Primary School, Oulton Broad

A Day At The Krusty Crab!

In my dreams every night
I see an underwater world filled with delight
SpongeBob makes his wonderful food
While Squidward is in a terrible mood.

They work all day in the Krusty Crab
As customers always try to grab
Even sharks come to eat
But they can't take a lovely seat.

People come to eat every day
But SpongeBob doesn't have enough time to stay
SpongeBob needs to get back home
So he can use his yellow comb.

Florence Minney (8)
Dell Primary School, Oulton Broad

In My Dreams Every Night

In my dreams every night
A fish had a fright
Dugongs doing the Griddy on the beach
White whales front flipping in the sea to teach
Orcas are having a feast
Great white sharks are a beast
Whales are in buildings playing games
Octopi are making flames
Penguins are swimming in Mexico
Squid are eating Domino's
Clownfish are driving cars
Birds are breaking prison bars
Silky sharks are eating meat
Sharks are drinking heat.

Jack Purser (8)
Dell Primary School, Oulton Broad

Untitled

In my dreams every night
I see an underwater world filled with delight
A family of clownfish, ten brothers and two sisters
Every day, all sisters and brothers go to school
A family of sharks join the school
One of them bullies me and his name is Juel
One night, he chases me out of the light
All the way to the trash where it becomes mash
But who is that?
It's my mother and Pat
As they distracted the shark
I swam as I am.

Saxon Turner (9)
Dell Primary School, Oulton Broad

Weird But Wonderful Dreams!

In my dreams every night,
An underwater kingdom is very bright,
Starfishes wearing a tutu in red,
Also having a party with bread.
SpongeBob going to meet a shark,
But having to go down in the dark,
They wanted to go and get dinner,
But found out that he was a lottery winner!
An octopus teaching me how to dance,
But all I do is have a prance,
What a dream to be under the ocean,
Lots of weird things but full of commotion!

Molly Jones (9)
Dell Primary School, Oulton Broad

In My Dreams Every Night

In my dreams, every night,
Spider crabs are glowing very bright.
Sea turtles howling, getting strikes,
Spider crabs whizzing on skybikes.

A jellyfish is driving a Lamborghini,
Clownfish are getting muddy.
Sharks surfing on the waves,
Stingrays hiding in a cave.

Manatees riding sea turtles,
An octopus chasing people.
A pufferfish playing on a Nintendo Switch,
A vampire squid turning on a light switch.

Alfie Doughty (7)
Dell Primary School, Oulton Broad

Dreams

In my dreams every night,
The spider crab does not want to fight,
As the mimic octopus does not want to bite,
They do an athlete course to see who will win,
The salmon, who is a coach who likes hiding in tins,
Smashes two together as they go whizz,
The shrimp blows bubbles that cause a fizz,
The spider crab acts like a king,
As the mimic octopus goes zing,
The spider crab wins the race, let's do it again!

Lucy Norman (8)
Dell Primary School, Oulton Broad

In My Dreams

In my dreams every night,
I see a dancer full of delight.
A dolphin dancing with glee,
A seahorse coming over for tea.

We're all having a fun party,
When *bang!* A shark came over to me,
And said he would also like some tea.

We thought we would order some dinner,
But instead, I found out I was a lottery winner.
An amazing place under the ocean,
Peculiar but full of commotion.

Meta Marcinkeviciute (9)
Dell Primary School, Oulton Broad

A Dream Under The Ocean

In my dreams every night,
I see an underwater kingdom full of delight.
Narwhals weaving through the sea,
But then SpongeBob is who I see.
He then runs away into the sea,
I thought I must go see.
But then it suddenly turned dark,
Then I had a ride on a shark.
We went to have some dinner,
I entered the lottery and I was a winner!
What a dream to have in the ocean,
Full of happiness and commotion.

Thea Wills (9)
Dell Primary School, Oulton Broad

Untitled

In my dreams every night
I see an underwater world filled with delight
Eels dressing up in a tuxedo and tie
Clownfish on a unicycle whizzing on by
Whales sat scoffing their dinner
A bright blue shark made a lottery winner
A seahorse playing a base guitar
An octopus driving a yellow sports car
What a wonderful place to be under the ocean
Suddenly, I heard a massive explosion
Boom!

Alfie Cutler (9)
Dell Primary School, Oulton Broad

In My Dreams Every Night

In my dreams, every night,
Ocean dreams spared bright.
A catfish going bowling,
Getting strikes,
Clownfish playing tennis,
Just for likes.

Stingrays bursting out
Funky dance moves,
Jellyfish learning Spanish
In his grooves.

Blobfish flying planes as a pilot,
Great white shark using the toilet.
Stingray flying a bright kite,
The penguins dancing, what a sight.

Millie Savannah Rose Cook (8)
Dell Primary School, Oulton Broad

My Dreams Every Night

A shark coming up to me saying I won the lottery
And a fish swaying doing some pottery
I can see a fish driving a sports car
I can see a fish wearing a bow tie
I can see a fish going to a party
I can see a cute fish driving a car
I can see a lemon fish going in a barn
I can see a hammerhead shark drinking some tea
I can see a clownfish eating some beans
I can see a starfish going to dance.

Rocco Dyke (8)
Dell Primary School, Oulton Broad

A Magical Ocean Comes Alive!

In my dreams every night
I always seem to get a fright
A wonderful ocean comes alive
While I get a massive surprise
Dolphins are playing with balls
While a starfish falls
In the Pacific, there are lots of strange sights full of commotion
It is very peaceful there
But some creatures don't really care
I think turtles are different colours
Just like others.

Esther Durrant (8)
Dell Primary School, Oulton Broad

In My Dreams Every Night

In my dreams every night,
I see a fish riding a bike,
A jellyfish roller skating,
And a clownfish trading,
A shark driving a car,
And a turtle looking at a star,
A seal standing,
A dolphin landing,
A starfish lying,
And a whale dumping,
An angelfish eating,
And an octopus dining,
A pufferfish puffing out, ready to sumo,
And a stingray winning Uno.

Kelsey Cook (8)
Dell Primary School, Oulton Broad

The Adventure Of A Lifetime

In my dreams every night,
I see my dog in sight,
Underwater friends waiting for me
A night-time adventure under the sea
A shark walks by
And I don't know why,
He's not making a commotion,
He must be in slow motion,
Suddenly he took Bruno and put him in a cage,
Then we went to save him, it filled me with rage,
I used my karate,
Then we had a party.

Ruby-Mai Curtis (9)
Dell Primary School, Oulton Broad

In My Dreams Every Night

In my dreams every night
Underwater with colours bright
Pufferfish dancing the waltz
Lobster tries to do a somersault
Squid still in prison
Dolphins going on a scary mission
Oyster drives a Lamborghini
Swordfish sitting on a sofa comfortably
Sharks on a zipline
Whales looking at the moonshine
Penguin moonwalking
Jellyfish with penguins, always stalking.

Ethan Zhang (8)
Dell Primary School, Oulton Broad

In My Dreams Every Night

In my dreams every night
Clownfish driving a pink sports car
Eels eat a lolly, the shape of a star
Dolphins brush their hair
While penguins swim from a bear
Stingrays powering the power line
While the shark looks for a place to dine
The seahorse watches the telly
So the pufferfish rubs its belly
I see a pufferfish breakdancing
I see a whale praying.

Isla Day (7)
Dell Primary School, Oulton Broad

In My Dreams Every Night

In my dreams every night,
My head like a night light,
Goldfish learning to do backflips,
While seahorses do amazing dips,
Dolphins spitting cool raps,
Whales getting lost and looking at their maps,
Again the sharks are playing tag,
Pufferfish going with their new bag,
Crabs doing a pinch competition,
Starfish waving one at a time like a superstition.

Ellie Folasade Davies (7)
Dell Primary School, Oulton Broad

In My Dreams Every Night

In my dreams every night
Fish flying with delight
Baby seals doing the baby dance
Penguins doing things like glancing
Orcas doing the head spinner
Clownfish throwing glitter
Orcas, clownfish parachuting to the moon
Stingrays holding a spoon
Whales biking
Squid striking
Clams boiling all night
Seashells at the bottom of the sea with light.

Katie Everett (7)
Dell Primary School, Oulton Broad

Hunters Of The Sea

In my dream every night I'm a pirate with a fright
And I'll catch you in the night
Me and my crew got a bite
And it was a neon shark, it was very bright
Because it was in the night
And we dived in the water to see what else we could find
We saw a sea dragon with an almighty fright
So we ran right away
We shot the dragon and drove away.

Ewan Watson (9)
Dell Primary School, Oulton Broad

Sea Dreams

In my dreams every night,
An octopus runs to the right,
A seahorse builds a house under the sea,
We can pack some food so they can eat with me,
I build a seaweed house for me to live in,
Then I see a scuba diver's skin,
Then I see a squid who is red,
He is sleeping in a bed,
After he looked at the sky,
They say, "Bye-bye!"

Roxy Harrod (8)
Dell Primary School, Oulton Broad

Untitled

In my dreams, every night,
A mermaid is in a terrible fright.
Octopi go to bed late at night,
The crab looks like he's going to fight.

But the starfish are getting tight,
The underwater kingdom is bright like a light.
An ocean appears to light,
Mermaids and octopi are tickling me,
But I don't mind, it's time for tea.

Darcie Tonks (9)
Dell Primary School, Oulton Broad

The Ocean

In my dreams every night,
A scuba diver swims with delight,
Crabs are swimming in the ocean,
Where there's lots of commotion,
Rocks started to crumble,
We took a bad tumble,
Stuck at the bottom of the ocean,
Looking for a special dolphin,
Mr Shark swims by and says, "Hi,"
And in a flash, they are flying high.

Matthew Hathaway (8)
Dell Primary School, Oulton Broad

Ocean Of My Dreams

Once upon a dream,
A whale was letting off steam.
The octopus let out ink,
It was very pink.

Angrily, a swordfish was having a brawl,
With a crab, very tall.
The school of fish,
Were holding a peculiar dish,
Made of shells,
There were ringing bells.
Once upon a dream,
Things weren't as they seem.

Harrison Maher (8)
Dell Primary School, Oulton Broad

Untitled

In my dreams every night,
Jellyfish hold a bright red kite,
Octopus eating an apple pie,
Pufferfish wearing a suit and tie,
Seahorse, Bob, as yellow as the sun,
Clownfish eating a cream-filled bun,
Sharks playing and catching a ball,
Stingrays looking at the blue wall,
This is where I live,
And I'm feeling alive.

Indiana Marjoram (8)
Dell Primary School, Oulton Broad

Me And My Pet Sea Tiger

In my dreams every night,
My pet sea tiger takes flight,
Diving into an underwater world,
Where walruses give,
Me and my sea tiger live,
There lives a sea turtle eating dinner,
A lemon shark becoming a lottery winner,
A football fish drinking some beer,
Pufferfish having a cheer,
In the ocean, I love the commotion.

Millie-Rose Bowman (9)
Dell Primary School, Oulton Broad

Below The Surface

In my dreams every night
The wonderful dolphin dances in the light
While the seahorse shines like a star
The sound of the water sways so far
The clownfish drives a car
The pufferfish is eating a chocolate bar
The beautiful squid has been climbing a cave
While the super shark saves
The great place of our imagination.

Lillie Cornwell (8)
Dell Primary School, Oulton Broad

In My Dreams

In my dreams every night,
Every day and night,
The lights are bright.

My friend and I play knights,
Day and night.

Seahorse dressed in a tuxedo and tie,
Jellyfish on roller skates
Whizzing, going by.

Sea fish sitting, eating their dinner,
A sea turtle becoming
A lottery winner.

Eva Hart (9)
Dell Primary School, Oulton Broad

Underwater World

In my dreams, every night,
I see an underwater world filled with delight.
Flying fish taking flight.
Crabs dance,
While seahorse prance.

Turtles play an electric guitar,
A pufferfish driving a green sports car.
A stingray meeting a squid at the park.
In the deep, dark ocean, it's very amazing.

Harry Youngs (8)
Dell Primary School, Oulton Broad

Underwater World Of Fright

In my dreams every night
I wake in a delightful world
There is a shell that is pearled
Seaweed talking
And a turtle walking
A clownfish smirking
And a squid lurking
A water snake slithering
Under a white shark shivering
I close my eyes and I go back
I will soon come back, but then that is that!

Sienna Whiteland (8)
Dell Primary School, Oulton Broad

In My Dreams Every Night

In my dreams every night an ocean appears,
In the ocean, an octopus tells me to dance!
But all I do is go to France,
Everyone takes a glance,
So I don't take a chance,
Bouncing, dancing jellyfish,
Mermaids waiting to grant my wish,
In the night sharks do fight,
When I'm trying to find the light.

Florence Vincent (9)
Dell Primary School, Oulton Broad

The Ocean Adventures

In my dreams every night,
A magical ocean comes alight,
Angelfish swim with multicoloured fins,
While joyful dolphins jump with their identical twins,
The deeper I go the more I feel at home,
The higher I go the more I feel alone,
There once was a girl who dreamed,
Now she is a scuba diver who gleams.

Scarlett Humphreys (9)
Dell Primary School, Oulton Broad

Under The Sea

In my dreams every night
I see a dragon having a fight
In the sea, splashing with glee
With my sister and dad screaming, "Whay!"
I sit in an underwater cinema chair
While breathing some air
I hate the lack of air
But I have a nice chair
The lionfish pride
Is affecting the tide.

Arlo Hender (8)
Dell Primary School, Oulton Broad

In My Dreams Every Night

In my dreams every night
I see an underwater world full of delight
Large football pitches
Fish gnawing their riches
Sea turtles and octopuses scoring goals
While the jellyfish and sharks are in the poles
I wonder when we'll win
They're making such a dish
In my underwater pitch.

Henley Wills (9)
Dell Primary School, Oulton Broad

A Running Water Poem

In my dreams every night
I seem to get a fright
Happy or not in the dark sea
I always seem to just be me
I feel happy under the sea
A manta ray likes to be clean
I saw a shark with a tail
I also saw a massive whale
I wish I saw a robot fish
But it was just a wish.

Oscar Edmunds (8)
Dell Primary School, Oulton Broad

Football Underwater

In my dreams every night,
I think of something that will be bright,
We score a goal,
And then I roll,
In the midnight zone,
I have a groan,
Seaweed swaying,
We're still playing,
Dolphins winning with us,
Squid spitting pus,
Ruby is not a noobie,
Shay will pay,
Dylan's just kiddin'.

Lenny Cole (9)
Dell Primary School, Oulton Broad

Football From Under The Sea

In my dreams every night,
Sea turns to light,
Blue soft waves dropping in the bright sand.

Underwater football is an amazing game,
Not so fast, it's very tame,
Messi and Ronaldo pass the pufferfish the ball,
A great white shark gives a team call.

William Copping (7)
Dell Primary School, Oulton Broad

Ocean Town

In my dreams every night
I see a very bright fish
Driving a motorbike
Sharks taking a big hike
Eels near an electric bar
Stingrays in a concert so far
Time to fly to the Pacific Ocean
So many different creatures
And a lot of potions.

Zaccai Sule (9)
Dell Primary School, Oulton Broad

Untitled

In my dreams every night
I can see a whale swimming with delight
Sea turtles swimming around
Crabs are sitting on the ground
Sea horses are dancing
Dolphins are prancing
What a remarkable sight
I have the best dreams all night.

Emilly Hammond (8)
Dell Primary School, Oulton Broad

The Ocean

In my dreams every night,
I swim and see colours bright,
I see fish swing left but not right,
But I see bread that has bites,
And sharks shining bright,
I will get pinched, I might,
Then I saw a kite,
And the string very tight.

Jasmine Dean (8)
Dell Primary School, Oulton Broad

The Underwater World

In my dreams every night
The deep blue sea is in my sight
With me and my friends we play
In time with a bang we go
To the sea with an ice cream
It falls, he cries in the sea while
His friend gets him another ice cream.

Ronan Langdale (8)
Dell Primary School, Oulton Broad

An Amazing Underwater Ocean World

In my dreams every night,
Turtles with colours so bright
Pufferfish in the sea
Angel sharks just like me
Lemon sharks passing by
Fish wearing a tie
Coral is alive
While people dive.

Brooklyn Withers (8)
Dell Primary School, Oulton Broad

The Night

In my dreams, every night,
I am amazed by the sight,
Although my toes are tickling with fright.

I found a wizard,
He said, "We need to stop the blizzard."

Charlotte King (8)
Dell Primary School, Oulton Broad

The Final

Here I am at the big game
Arriving on the plane
I drive in my car
Past the bar
I arrive at the pitch
It felt like I was rich

When I was training
It was heavily raining
Here we are at the start
Someone said my football is art
I saw fouls, cards, offsides and goals
Everyone was playing their roles

It was near the end
We had to defend
Finally, the whistle was blown
Something we wanted we finally own
There it is, the trophy
I was standing next to the goalie.

With smiles on our faces, we lifted it high
Then we waved to the crowd goodbye
We were singing and dancing all night

We felt so bright
'Til we were back again.

Amelie Holden (11)
Flakefleet Primary School, Fleetwood

Fulfill Your Dreams

F ulfill your dreams today,
U nique is what they are,
L asting long in your memory,
F or you to become that star,
I nside you is your special dream,
L onging to break out,
L asting inside your thoughts.

Y ou only have to give it a shout,
O ver time you can fulfill your dreams,
U topia is where you will find them,
R emembering that special one.

D eveloping deep within your mind,
R eflecting on that special dream,
E ach and every day,
A lways thinking I have a dream,
M ay it come true today,
S o what is your special dream?

Brody Wilson (10)
Flakefleet Primary School, Fleetwood

Different Dream Worlds

One moment you are swinging,
In the magnificent jungle.
Then next you're swimming with turtles,
Then you're jumping over hurdles.

You've got low gravity in space
You're running at a world-record pace.
Then you're soaring sky-high.
Then you're on the beach getting dry.

Out of nowhere
You're falling off a building
You wake up sweatin', you've got a foggy mind.
You clear your mind then the amazing experience that seemed so real,
Well, now you can experience it, in the real deal.

Freddie William Butterfield (10)
Flakefleet Primary School, Fleetwood

Desired Jobs

Have you ever had a dream about your future?
Have you had a dream about your desired job?
About being a doctor or a chef
Or even working at KFC?
Well my dream is to be a footballer
Scoring goals, yeah that's my goal in life!
Making a lifetime amount of money
And eating lots of honey
Like a bee, I swarm the ball
No one can stop me
My feet are like rockets
My head is like a header machine
Then the sun rose
I was trying not to wake up
But then I remembered if I try
I can do it until I die.

Ralph Broadbent (10)
Flakefleet Primary School, Fleetwood

Clowns

Clowns everywhere I look,
I've got no money, it's all been took.
Clowns, they're everywhere!
Some don't have hair!

Some are everywhere I go,
Along down the road.
I skip down that road sometimes,
I nearly break a hip sometimes!

I stumble upon a circus
I find someone named Bertus.

I run and run, he's the scariest clown!
Find a forest and get lost,
But don't find a town...

Ellouise-Mai Wright (10)
Flakefleet Primary School, Fleetwood

Life

Don't let the
Vague give
Blindness in your eyes
Let your heart illuminate
You won't last in this life not reading
Between the lines and getting conquered with
Pain and all those hurtful cries.

This life ain't perfect in mind
A thought to keep
There are times you have no choice but to pray.

For events may quickly flip
Or else you'll lose grip
And far away you'll slip.

Miley-Rae Birch (11)
Flakefleet Primary School, Fleetwood

The Rustle Of The Night

Me, Brook, Velvet, Mark and Jessica
Were walking down the road like toads
We fell into a tunnel and Velvet crumbled her bubble
She screamed and they were in trouble
We were trapped in a funnel.
We found a ladder that gave Brook a splinter
Jessica gave her a plaster,
Mark had some bark.
Jessica tunnelled back and Brook wasn't there
I found a monster
So I started to pray and got my way.

Megan Crane (11)
Flakefleet Primary School, Fleetwood

The Famous Dancer

I dance with the flow
I know when to flow
Shoes clicking and tapping like the rain dripping
I look above, I see stars in my mind
Stars, stars twinkling like a bird flapping their wings
As bright as the moon ticking
I lift my feet like a sunrise
And take deep breaths and put my feet back on the ground
I hear pictures, photographers, paparazzi
Whoever's reading this...
I'm famous!

Aniyah Stokes (11)
Flakefleet Primary School, Fleetwood

Football Dream

Football is a sport of roughness
Although it takes some skill
It just takes practice to get over that massive hill
But like they say
Practice makes perfect in any way
The practice might get rather hectic
As people start to get frustrated
After the game, you sure will be glad
It is not about the fame
The game is for fun
If you get it done
You will be better than ever.

Kacie Brooke (11)
Flakefleet Primary School, Fleetwood

Clown

Brooke and I were in the fairground playing games
Then I heard a scary voice shouting our names
I patted Brooke on the shoulder and told her about the voice
We cautiously looked around but that was a bad choice
We looked under the hook-a-duck game
Then I heard whispers whispering my name
Me and Brooke sharply turned our heads
We screamed and shouted, hoping it was a dream.

Velvet Cunningham (11)
Flakefleet Primary School, Fleetwood

The Nightmare In My Head

I wake up in the pitch-black of my room.
I get up out of bed, feeling weird and confused.
I walk up to my dresser.
I open the drawer and here is what I see,
A bunch of tiny eyes looking at me.
I fall to the floor in horror and fright,
I crawl away with not much delight.
I hide under my bed hoping to be safe.
But there was a knife that could take my life anyway.

Brooke Nullall (10)
Flakefleet Primary School, Fleetwood

Rock Show

One day at a concert,
A sniffled, snuffled man named Dan
Sniffled and sneered towards a metal guitar
And played a staggering and stubborn beat
The guitars screamed in pain
As I leapt away in the destruction of the crowd
Trying to find my way out of the crowd to get out
I woke up
No stage, no crowd, nothing.

Jenson Jessop (11)
Flakefleet Primary School, Fleetwood

Things Take Time

The efforts you are making today,
The tasks you are doing,
Rarely produce instant results.
Be patient,
Watch, make adjustments,
Make a plan and plant a seed,
That takes time as well.
Keep up what you are doing,
I'm proud!
The world seems to be in a rush,
But I choose to remain still!

Jasmine Gardener (11)
Flakefleet Primary School, Fleetwood

The Land Of The Monsters

On an abandoned island,
In the middle of the sea,
Dinosaurs were running around,
With monsters chasing me.

I looked around the place,
No place to run.
A monster then said,
"There's nowhere to go, you've had your fun."

I carried on running,
There was an old shack.
I knocked on the door,
There was a big thwack.

An old man scared me,
I let out a scream.
Slowly opening my eyes,
It was sadly just a dream.

Danish Mohammed Ali (10)
Goldbeaters Primary School, Edgware

Life

The sky is dark at night
And shadows are watching me,
Oh how can I sleep if the world is watching me?
So I tell myself this is life,
Life that we waste every day
And I ask myself are we dead or alive?
Oh I try.

People are dead, we are depressing,
But can we even enjoy simple blessings?
So I tell myself this is life,
Life we isolate ourselves from each other,
Life we waste every day,
Life we can't enjoy
But life we can live today.

Salma Farah (11)
Goldbeaters Primary School, Edgware

My School, My Pride

My school, my pride,
Where we have a wonderful school inside.
We read, we write,
And make our futures bright.
We learn to respect, not to neglect,
We learn to accept,
Not to expect.
We laugh, we cry,
And learn to keep our anger inside.
We play, we study,
With our best buddies!
Respect elders, obey parents.
Become sincere and mature,
Is the habitat we learn...
And that's what we call,
My school, my pride.

Zainab Dahir (10)
Goldbeaters Primary School, Edgware

Nightmare

Shadows on the wall
Creepy ghouls on the door
Nightmare
People's life damaging
Time changing
Nightmare

Goblins and cats
Taking one's soul
Nightmare
Ghosts and zombies
Screaming as they stroll
Nightmare

Upon a window sill
A rat froze so still
Nightmare
Murderous beasts
And brains for midnight feasts
Nightmare.

Elisa Sheikhi (11)
Goldbeaters Primary School, Edgware

Sweetyland Dream

Thair wis this dream a gey silly yin 'n' ah hate th' dentist.
No, let me tell ye about it.
See ah wis fleet asleep.
Ah wis in this Sweetyland.

'N' ah heard this swish swish sound ah wis terribly scared
Bit ah tak three steps tae forward 'n' a'm a rascal sae
Ah jist jumped back then ah hit mah haun and gave it arub 'n' skelped mah coupon.

"Ah deserve that," ah said.

Sae ah git tae th' bush, weel cotton candy bush
Ah pat mah haun ben ah could feel a fluffy feeling.
Ah pulled it oot 'n' twas a fluffy bunny, whoa! Ah git a bunny!
Shouting 'n' lifting it in th' air I'm tae ca' it snowy! Yer a white bunny.

Ah I looked around the world I'm in and it is full af sweets,
But I'm actually sleepwalking and eating marshmallows.

But in yin meenit I'm getting two teeth oot, so I got two cavities.

Harper Duncan (9)
Laurieston Primary School, Laurieston

My Worst Nightmare

As I am walking through the forest to the park,
I feel something brush past me.
I see a murky shadow in the distance,
I was all alone but now I'm not so sure.
I hear a voice calling my name,
I don't have a choice but to keep walking.
Then I hear a scream,
I want to investigate.
Lucky for me I brought a torch to show me the way.
Then suddenly the murky, mysterious shadow comes towards me,
And I realise it's a clown.
The clown starts to chase me, I run and see my town,
I sprint up to my house, hoping that my door is open.
But to my surprise it is broken.
Anyway, I sprint in, hiding behind my sofa,
Hoping I won't die.

Oscar McRobbie (9)
Laurieston Primary School, Laurieston

My Dream

In th' best dream ever
A'm a famous wee bairn
Surroundit by people's bright flashing cameras.

A'm in front o'a casino
Wi' mah bodyguards beside me
An' wains asking for mah autograph.

A'm travellin' thru th' casino
An' ev'rybody stops 'n' stares
An' I ga'an hurl ah casino wheel
An' ah win 10 billion poonds!

Instead o' continuin' tae gamble
Ah use th' dosh ta gie th'a bin howker a home
An' used th' rest o' th' dosh tae hav a go at solvin' wo'ld hunger.

Arran Blue (9)
Laurieston Primary School, Laurieston

Me And James Tavernier

Me and James Tavernier play fur the Rangers
Very famous playing in the Champions League
It's 1-1, we are playing against Celtic.

We git a penalty 'n' am taking it
Could we score tae make it 2-1?

We dae kid, we keep it 2-1
But they score in the last minute
It's off tae penalties.

Could anybody score?
Na it's off tae penalties.

Am taking the fifth, it's 4-4 on penalties
If we score we win 'n' ah scored!
We win!

Jamie Smith (9)
Laurieston Primary School, Laurieston

The Aether

Ah thought ah woke up wance
Bit ah wis just a dunce
Ah wis in a magical place
Boon th' sky 'n' sand.

Thare wis tons o' rice
Gladly na mice
There is bunnies that made ye fly
Heich in the sky.

It's aye bricht in th' sky
That's how come ye dinnae need a light
Thare is temples ilka whaur
Protected wi' a hoard o' bears.

Tis filled wi' gummy sweets 'n' a ton o' meats.

Alexander Vasilev (9)
Laurieston Primary School, Laurieston

The Titanic Blast

One day the Titanic left the dock
As the Britannic honked
The ship boosters took the ship
40 metres into the air
As the boats were getting there
The vessel blasted forward
The ship's front compartment opened
To show a disco ball
As the captain called, "Hold on
We'll drive at dawn,"
A massive rocket shot right past
As it turned halfway past
Slowly the ship landed in water
And then sank.

Benjamin Mackintosh (9)
Laurieston Primary School, Laurieston

Football

F or this game, I am against Hamilton.
O ne more goal would make me win the Ballon d'Or.
O ne day left until the player gets announced, and it's me.
T he last minute of the game now.
B etter try harder, we need to win this.
A ll the players on the pitch are really good.
L ast game I scored the winning goal.
L ast game in the Champions League, I won.

Eli Paterson (9)
Laurieston Primary School, Laurieston

Wandy And The Wizard

D reaming of wizards is my favourite thing of all
R eally my dream is to be in the Great Hall like Harry
E ven when I try to talk the laughter inside me keeps it from coming out
A mazing things are waiting for me to rise to destiny
M y trusty Wandy will always be by my side, even if I'm fighting a wizard
S ometimes when I eat at the Great Hall, I eat too much.

Matthew Darrell (9)
Laurieston Primary School, Laurieston

The Zombies

Wance a fungus came 'n' teak ower.
Then cam' tea see 'n' a' body git taken.
But it a' started in 1895, noo tis 2024 a' o' us died bit two fowk.
Thare aye oot there wi' ur hawp is there hauns.
By noo ye wid o' thought there gaen.
Then cricket cam a' th' world is gaen.
Bit tis nae ower yit tea two fowk ur aye gaun.

Emily Meiklejohn (9)
Laurieston Primary School, Laurieston

The Space Staircase

D reaming of building a new staircase to space all by myself.
R ockets racing and shooting through the sky.
E ven aliens fly in their flying saucers.
A massive asteroid came towards the staircase.
M ars is the red planet.
S unlight is shining through the clouds.

Charlotte Dewar (9)
Laurieston Primary School, Laurieston

Paradise Land

P aradise in the making
E legant is the style these days
R oyalty for queen corn
F lamingos in the big summer pool
E verything you can imagine, except scary stuff
C ats and dogs everywhere
T rees everywhere, like palm and blossom.

Freya Sturrock (9)
Laurieston Primary School, Laurieston

Space Football

I was in space, minding my own business
Suddenly I saw something in the distance
I saw a figure in the distance and I could barely see it
The person was small like a ball
So I tried to get a closer look
To find out who he was
I recognised his face and had to pause.

Leo McArthur (9)
Laurieston Primary School, Laurieston

The Flying Turtle

D reaming about flying
R acing through the sky
E arlier in the day
A mazing adventures
M oney floating by
S peeding across the sky.

Summer Begg (9)
Laurieston Primary School, Laurieston

A Braw Athlete

Ah kin see a mackle castle
A water 'n' muckle
Bonny butterflies flying about
And a'm wi' my BFF
A'm in a land cried Athlete Land.

Laila Stewart (9)
Laurieston Primary School, Laurieston

Believe And Dream

B elieve in what you think
E veryone should believe
L ove your dreams
I love my dreams and hopes
E ven little kids should love and believe
V illain people and everyone in my family and we all dream and believe
E ven my teddies believe and you should too

A nd if you don't believe or dream, you should try it because it's amazing
N an, Dad, Mum, Grandad and cousins believe in magic, believe you will feel amazing
D reams and beliefs

D reaming can be great you can
R emember what you dreamed and believed in and think about how it makes you feel
E xamples are dreaming if you were in a magical land
A nd you were a time-traveller and looked into the past to see what they did.
M aybe if you believe and dream you will never feel or be alone!

But all of this started in a dream!

Kaddy Nyanfora (8)
Perry Court E-ACT Academy, Hengrove

The Fate Of The Mermaid Princess

Under the Caribbean Sea, in cool waters blue,
Was a mermaid princess.
With ebony curls and pearl-white skin,
With a long, sparkly tail with crystals down to the fin.

She was loved by the queen and she was loved by the king,
Her favourite hobby was to sing.
Her voice was enchanting and desired by all,
Especially by the sea demon called Norwall.

With slimy tentacles and huge, black spots on his back,
He lurks in the shipwreck, plotting her kidnap.
Guarded by sharks was the royal treasure,
Which holds the key to her power.

As darkness approached, across the ocean floor,
The sea demon got closer and went straight for the palace door.
With a flick of a tentacle, the princess was gone,
Transported to prison, where her days and nights were long.

As the sun rose in the sky, and the ocean was still,
I opened my eyes, darkness was all around me,
My bed was cold and damp,
Unable to sing myself a lullaby, not even a sound,
I'm trapped! Someone help, please!
I am the mermaid princess,
I will survive!

Zara Davey (8)
Perry Court E-ACT Academy, Hengrove

My Best Dream Ever!

Once I drifted off to sleep I had a dream,
It was when I met a monster and he had superpowers.
We spent lots of time together, we even liked to play,
He could teleport to London and even the USA.
And I remember he once teleported to my grandma's house.
The monster got his superpowers from a magic potion,
And when the potion started to work it caused a huge commotion.
He gave me a super magic potion, I teleported everywhere I wanted,
His powers were amazing, I really wanted those powers for the rest of my life.
When he got bored, he would teleport to different places,
The monster had a new pair of shoes which were laces,
And every six minutes he had to stop and tie them up.
My monster had a dog that died called Pup,
I got sad but I pulled myself together and said goodbye.
Then I woke up with all different feelings, but mostly happy.

Sophie Stratford (8)
Perry Court E-ACT Academy, Hengrove

Lost In My Dreams

Every time I close my eyes late at night
I see a bright light in my sight
Leading me to where it is right
Then I see snow which is so white
Crunch, crunch, crunch, walking, holding my arms so tight.

I hear a rustle in the bush
I stop, I'm scared, I hear a whoosh,
I look down, it's my dog Willow who followed me
I told her to hush
We kept on walking but the floor is full of slush
We must be careful so we don't rush.

I feel lost, I don't know where to go
I'm in a forest, a magical land, I look up and see a glow
I need to wake up, I need to go home, but it's taking too slow
Is the glow the way home? Quick Willow, let's go
We rush, we run, *whoosh*
My eyes open, I'm home
I'm safe, I'm no longer lost.

Laya Alznati (10)
Perry Court E-ACT Academy, Hengrove

The Final Score

When I go to sleep at night
I shut my eyes really tight
I start to dream, I wish it was real
I got the contract, I signed the deal
I'm number 7 for Chelsea FC
I can't believe it, go me!
Walking out through the tunnel, the crowds roar
I hope I score
The match starts, I get the ball
Run past the defenders and set up a goal
1-0 to Chelsea, up the blues!
There is no way we're going to lose
Sterling passes me the ball, I run with it
I shoot, I score!
Top bins it is, now let's get one more
Before the match is over my mum wakes me up
I want ten more minutes, but I'm out of luck
I'll continue my dreams tonight
When I close my bedroom door
I'll shut my eyes really tight
And see the final score.

Louie Phillips (7)
Perry Court E-ACT Academy, Hengrove

My Magical Dream

My magical dream begins on a farm,
Where no one meant any harm.
These animals weren't normal though,
They could glow!
Every night, they would give out a light,
Indeed it was very bright.
The light was very powerful,
And they decided to go near a bull.
The bull didn't like it,
Not one bit.
The bull ignored them for a while,
And just put on a fake smile.
Eventually, the bull told them about how he got annoyed by the light,
And the animals didn't do it again during the night.
The animals become friends,
And, no, they don't pretend.
They love spending time together,
Like they're siblings and share the same mother.
They never get into fights,
And especially, they never bite.

Tara Nasiri Khanghahi (9)
Perry Court E-ACT Academy, Hengrove

The Best Dream Ever!

I had a dream, just last night,
But this one felt amazing right?
So listen up and you will see,
Just what happened to Keira and me.

We got awarded from our school,
For being truly outstanding pupils,
But this was just the very start,
Where we're heading next will warm your hearts.

Buckingham Palace was the place to be,
The King waiting for Kiera and me.
For all our work, he gave us so much praise,
That we'll never forget for days and days.

But the best bit was yet to come,
A surprise for us at the Royal kingdom.
Little Mix waiting for us, for me?
Keira and me were as happy as can be.

Summerlee Filer (9)
Perry Court E-ACT Academy, Hengrove

Once Upon A Dream

Oh how I love to dream every night,
I fly on a unicorn in my dreams,
But when I wake up,
Nothing is as it seems.
I fly above the trees,
I can spy some bumblebees.
When I look down I see tiny cars,
When I look up I see shining stars.
I keep going up with my unicorn,
Staring at her beautiful horn.
I start to notice the higher we go,
My unicorn has a shimmering bow.
As we begin to travel down,
My happy face turns to a frown.
Goodbye my unicorn, my special friend,
I hoped this dream would never end.
I wish to see you another night,
Because that would be such a delight.

Mariana Vicentim (8)
Perry Court E-ACT Academy, Hengrove

Beautiful Princess

B e nice and kind
E legant and cute
A nd dress up pretty as a queen
U se your beauty brain for gaining knowledge
T ea time with your friends
I mprove your dance moves
F eel confident in yourself
U nderstand people's problems
L ove everyone.

P lay new games
R emember your duties
I magine yourself where you love to go
N urture the plants
C aring for everyone
E njoy every moment
S atisfy with what you have
S imply live your life joyfully.

Pritanshi Gundemoni (6)
Perry Court E-ACT Academy, Hengrove

White Ponies

Beyond the trees was a bright, shimmering light
I was going for my evening walk when it was night
As I walked towards it there weren't donkeys
To my surprise, it was twinkling white ponies

I chose the pony that was as bright as the sun
When we reached home, I gave it a bun
The next day, I took my pony to school
It was too hot, so I took it to cool

The life of a pony is amazing!
It was lunchtime at school, but my pony was missing
As I returned home, pony said, "Peek-a-boo"
For the safety of my pony, we handed her over to the zoo.

Brihati Gundemoni (7)
Perry Court E-ACT Academy, Hengrove

Oh No

I walked past an eerie forest,
Crunch, crunch, crunch,
I saw a boy who said his name was Larris.
Ticking in my head I heard a creepy chorus,
I questioned, was that my best friend, Morris?
Aggressively he grabbed my hand and said, "Come with me now."
This definitely wasn't Morris, but how?
I had to go right now,
I had to sprint, would he allow?
I saw a cat in the tree, it purred, meow,
Me and so-called Morris had a humungous row.

Maddison-Leigh Pearce (10)
Perry Court E-ACT Academy, Hengrove

Sweet Dreams

S leep tight, don't let the bed bugs bite
W e will see you in the morning
E xciting adventures await
E xtraordinary things can happen
T ell me all about it

D reams are always possible
R emember to kiss me goodnight
E arly nights mean more time to dream
A lways dream big
M ums and dads are always near
S leep tight, don't let the bed bugs bite.

Layla Stuckes (10)
Perry Court E-ACT Academy, Hengrove

The Midnight Sky

In my dream I dream about a midnight sky
That has pixie dust for clouds
And potions float through the sky
I see a land that is made from cotton candy
And has candy for plants
I hear fresh colours
And see music being played
Vegetables are mis-spoken of
As well as work
I dream of a place where anything comes true
And flowers grow on hair
This is what I dream of every night
When I go to bed.

Yasmina-Roberta Suciachi (10)
Perry Court E-ACT Academy, Hengrove

In My Dreamland

In my mind as I drift to sleep,
I fall into a land where shadows can't creep.
It's where unicorns run free,
Mermaids explore the sea.
And there is no such thing,
As a very bad dream.
No monsters can hide,
No mean brothers can fight.
The days are bright,
Not a bad thing in sight.
In this land you don't cry,
In this land you can fill your tummy with warm apple pie.

Josie Gill (7)
Perry Court E-ACT Academy, Hengrove

The Jungle Dream

Once before in my dream,
I woke up in a jungle near a stream,
I saw my friend, very forlorn,
And I saw some leaves, but they were torn,
I was shocked, also worried,
So me and my friend hurried,
We started to search, lots of times,
Then we saw some lovely vines,
We then thought we could escape,
Then me and my friend found a tape,
And then I was awake.

Scarlet Smart (9)
Perry Court E-ACT Academy, Hengrove

Dream Horse

Hooves jump over my head,
Whilst I dream in bed,
As they're riding on the golden lanes,
I find their colourful manes,
From another planet, they come,
I never want this time to be done,
Every night I leave out oats,
Because in this cold they need strong coats,
But sadly one night they disappear,
Perhaps they'll come again next year.

Beau Chapman (10)
Perry Court E-ACT Academy, Hengrove

My Dreams

Unicorns fly
Fairies as well
The dancers wished they could too
I'm so confused, my bestie too

Dragons sleep
The monsters peep
While the spiders creep
The scary dolls look so cheap

The wizard casts a spell
Making the pirate smell
The clown doesn't smell better
This place needs a new writer, it's me!

Disini Pallwela (7)
Perry Court E-ACT Academy, Hengrove

Multiple Me's

Every night
I have a fright
I am lost
In the woods
I see many trees
And many me's
They chase me until I'm tired
They chase me until I fall
I cry and cry until
They stop
Then they drop
And then disappear
I cough and cough but then I see smoke
Oh, I just woke.

Chanade Sheridan (10)
Perry Court E-ACT Academy, Hengrove

Swifty World

Pink bodysuit brushing past
1989, Lover, Red, Speak Now
All in the most successful section
Meeting Taylor Swift, oh what a dream
Brushing through the clouds
All dancing around
Singing Shake It Off
And enjoying the day
What a slay!
Being with my sisters
Closely gathered around.

Freya Topp (11)
Perry Court E-ACT Academy, Hengrove

Nightmare

What's a nightmare?
Every night you get a little scare
What's a nightmare?
That scary picture in your head
Always leading you to dread
What's a nightmare?
Always dark at night
You get that little fright
That's a nightmare.

Freya Borsay (9)
Perry Court E-ACT Academy, Hengrove

Winged Horse

I wish...
That I could meet a winged horse named Pegasus,
With white, creamy fur
That always flies through the blue sky,
Also loves to eat fruits to make her beautiful.
And she lives in a colourful rainbow
And loves to meet her horse friends.

L M Dinugi (10)
Perry Court E-ACT Academy, Hengrove

The Dancers And The Magical Feeling

Far, far away,
There was a bay.
Where dancers would dance,
Birds would glance.
With a tip of an eye,
We spotted a guy.
With a swish of a wand,
There was a pond.
I got this magical feeling,
It was appealing.

Mollie Parker (11)
Perry Court E-ACT Academy, Hengrove

The Day Everyone's Teeth Turned Green

The day everyone's teeth turned green,
I tried to scrub them clean,
I didn't succeed,
So I ran at high speed,
But I knew it was only a dream.

Hazel Autumn Lewin Gilbert (8)
Perry Court E-ACT Academy, Hengrove

Once Upon A Dream

The fire flickers like the sun
And it disappeared and the candles danced in the moonlight
And the sky was dark, as deep as the ocean
And the moon smiled a cheesy grin
And the stormy sea roared like thunder and lightning
The cloud was like a snow cloud
And my house was made of carrot cake
And the rocks were made of chocolate
And the roof tiles are made of rainbow colours
And my door is made of toffee
And I have superpowers
And I am in a cave and I am on the monsters
And I am in a dinosaur park
And I want to be a football player
But I am swimming in the ocean
And I saw a monster and a shark coming towards me
And I tried to get to shore
But something happened to me
And teleported to World War II
And I went to war in the army
Fighting the Germans and Hitler
I went to a concentration camp.

James Clarck (9)
Regis Manor Primary School, Milton Regis

The Dream Of Fairies

Once upon a dream, where moonbeams softly gleam
In a realm where fairies waltz an enchanted scene
Whisper of magic, through the night they stream
A ballet of stardust, a celestial dream.

In the tapestry of night, where wishes take flight
Fairies dance on petals, bathed in silvery light
The gossamer wings, a shimmering delight
As they weave tales of wonder, in the safest of night

Through the meadows of slumber, where dreams intertwine
Fairies twirl and pirouette, a celestial design
Stars above witness their enchanting incline
A kind ballet, pure and divine

Tiny feet grace the eternal stage
Moonlight giggles in a magical cage
Each family's laughter, a melody of sage
Creating ripples in the cosmic page.

John Olamiko (9)
Regis Manor Primary School, Milton Regis

Dream Or Nightmare

D ancing sunlight came over me
R unning, free animals came past me
E veryone having fun and being kind
A ll of the world, happy and calm
M usic like the breeze was tranquil.

O ver the hills came the wind
R an away the happiness.

N ow the darkness filled the air
I n the world, no peace remained
G hosts filled the world, instead of the fairies
H otter became the fire as it turned angrier
T hud! Lightning and thunder appeared
M ore and more frightening things happened
A rgh! A fierce dragon was following me
R oar! came a sound from behind
E verything turned black.

Edmile Valantinaviciute (9)
Regis Manor Primary School, Milton Regis

In The Dreams

In the dreams of a girl,
There are dolls and unicorns,
With lots of pink and white,
But all can be different,
In a boy's dream.

In the dreams of a boy,
There are dinos and planes,
With lots of blue and green,
But all can be different,
In a dog's dreams.

In a dog's dream,
There are treats and treats,
That they will devour,
But all can be different,
In a cat's dream.

In a cat's dream
There are cat treats,
And sofas they will scratch,
But all can be different,
In my dreams.

In my dreams,
There are lots of things,
That goes through my head,
Hopes and dreams,
That I hope
Will come true soon.

Teegan Charles (11)
Regis Manor Primary School, Milton Regis

Dreamers

D riving through mysterious deserts, dancing with talking animals that don't exist
R acing with famous people like Mo Farrah, running up mountains like Mount Everest.
E xploring Egyptian caves that were forgotten, and experiencing a flight with magical animals.
A chieving world records that were never beaten, amazingly find buried treasure
M astering a backflip, mummy finding
E ating the world's best traditional food, exactly throwing a dart at the target.
R iding chariots, reading Belle's books
S inging in the O2, swimming with sharks

Readers and dreamers are leaders.
So let your imagination run wild
And discover your dreams.

Josette Kusi (9)
Regis Manor Primary School, Milton Regis

My Dream

The sun shines bright,
In the beautiful daylight,
Only me, myself and I,
Will see the wonderful sight,
At the end of the rainbow, what should there be?
Jewellery, candy, or just a tall tree?
As I slowly walk closer, I can start to see,
What there will be waiting for me,
The end of the rainbow, oh wow!
It's even cooler than I expected it to be!
Unicorns, fairies, diamonds and more!
Gold coins, little elves, everything I adore!
Sadly I woke up hoping there would be
Another dream like this in the future,
Maybe!

Alexandra Ciurca (10)
Regis Manor Primary School, Milton Regis

Football

Every time I dream bright,
As the footballers play right.
As the footballers move,
I groove.
I remember when I was ten,
I watched amazing men.
The ball moves as if it has a mind of its own,
I get angry and moan.
Saka's feet move faster,
As if he is a master.
While football is a good sport,
There are some other sorts.
Reach your goal it's high,
But you're really nigh.
If you work hard,
You will outsmart.
As I sit with my supportive family,
I have fun with them.

Christabella Akiri (10)
Regis Manor Primary School, Milton Regis

Spooky School

I had a dream,
In the classroom,
A monster may loom,
Books are everywhere,
But there's nothing in there.
A skeleton baby lay in the chair,
He gave me a scare,
I chose to stay,
Because I felt okay,
On the board was writing in chalk,
I knew the rebels would always talk.
Souls were whispering,
I was looking,
We chose to leave,
As nerves ran up my sleeve.
When we left, I was happy.
I told my daddy.

Ellie Sheridan (9)
Regis Manor Primary School, Milton Regis

Dreams And Nightmares

I have a dream,
I have a nightmare,
My eyes close tight at the seams,
Dancing, sounds, a chill down my spine,
Is it a dream or nightmare this time,
I open my eyes to peek above,
I try to whisper but out pops a shout.
Fairies or dragons or big scary clowns,
I lay down inside my bed,
Off to Imagination Land in my head.

Amelia Maitland (9)
Regis Manor Primary School, Milton Regis

Once Upon A Dream

Once upon a dream,
There was a girl with a scheme,
Her plan was freedom,
From her horrible kingdom,
Her name was crazy, it was Daisy,
They say she's sweet,
She thinks they are lying,
Because when she doesn't get her way she starts crying,
Her plan was to climb,
But when it was time...
Bang!
Her mum bursts through the door,
The suitcase falls to the floor,
"Are you running away? Please stay!" said Mum,
Just to make it clear,
If she stayed she would survive,
She said she would stay until that night,
But she prepared to start a fight.

Hollie Knight (11)
Ruskin Academy, Wellingborough

The Future

Walking down a future street,
My family and I saw a fleet
Of future cars flying past.
Super shiny, super fast.

Zooming, hovering, speeding by,
The future cars filled the sky.
It made me feel quite excited,
Full of wonder and feeling delighted.

Future sights and future sounds
Everything was different all around.
Was it a dream or was it real?
I didn't know how to feel.

Walking in a future dream,
Can I believe what I have seen?
Is it a sight of things to be?
It looked very strange to me.

Charlie Stronach (8)
Ruskin Academy, Wellingborough

Gymnast's Dream

A girl who adores gymnastics,
I think it's really fantastic,
I can do a cartwheel,
It's not really a big deal.
In a competition, I wish I could do a backbend,
On TikTok, I saw that trend.
I have been practising for three to four years,
I have many dance peers.
Also, I can do a handstand,
Stand, then land!

Suddenly, I won, I was astonished,
I won a medal, all perfectly polished,
Even a gold, amazing trophy.
Did I win against Sophie?
However, I woke up in bed,
"What an awesome dream!" I said.

Oliwia Dziecielska (10)
Ruskin Academy, Wellingborough

The Magical Wonderland

Coming into a world with wizards,
Who could turn people to lizards,
Dragons flying in the sky,
Going to the moon and saying bye,
High in the mountains, hyenas are running,
Ready to hunt, they are coming,
Builders building wrecked domes,
Made out of dinosaur bones,
Monsters hiding under the bed,
Some of them are real scared,
Up in the circus all around,
You may find many clowns,
In the ocean, oh so deep,
Mermaids sing till they're asleep
In a world so magical,
Nothing is impossible...

Patricia Zdrinca (10)
Ruskin Academy, Wellingborough

I Woke Up

I wake up and everything is a dream
The light is a beam.
My arms are as dirty as a rock.
My dream was about living on a dock.

Have I dreamed all week?
My brother is calling to play hide-and-seek.
I don't want to move,
I feel so soothed.

I am desperate for warmth,
My arms reach for warmth.
I need somebody to help.
It feels like I am trapped! Help!

I feel like a cookie,
I am a low rank in this game,
Especially a rookie.
Today is my big day.

Holly Maginnis (10)
Ruskin Academy, Wellingborough

My Wonderland

D inosaurs flying
R oaming the Earth
E ating all they see
A nd living their life's worth
M any magical dreams
S tarting with me

W ith my mum and my aunties all flying free
I feel happy and magical
T he fairies and unicorns all dancing with glee
H elping those who need it with you and me

M y wonderland
E scaping my reality.

Oceana Munton (10)
Ruskin Academy, Wellingborough

Cats

Cats are cute and fluffy,
They can also be scruffy,
Cats are the best,
Though they can be a pest.

In all shapes and sizes, they come,
Cats think snuggles and kisses are fun,
Cats make really good pets,
And don't like to get wet.

They can be lions,
They play in dandelions,
They can also be tigers,
They are blocked by wires.

Maia Rickett-Browne (10)
Ruskin Academy, Wellingborough

My Dapper Dragon

In my dreams every night
I see a dragon flying left and right
Sometimes I get scared as a cat
Because my dragon wears a hat
He often visits and says hello
His jacket is a lovely yellow
In my dreams, I am a wizard for the King
So I ride on my dragon and we sing.

Leon Bailey (10)
Ruskin Academy, Wellingborough

My Horse Riding Dream

M aking hay nets
Y ay! It's time to ride.

H orses walking, trotting and cantering
O n my horse and ready to go
R iding is so fun
S pooked, oh no!
E ating yummy carrots.

R eady to go on the road
I cy cold weather, I can't ride
D eciding to trot or canter
I love horses
N othing can stop me
G etting my helmet on.

D oing the mucking out
R ide into the distance
E xciting!
A massive puddle
M aking sure my horses get all my love.

Grace Harvey (8)
Springbank Academy, Eastwood

I Want To Be A Footballer

I want to be a footballer
I'm practising my skills
I'm doing lots of fitness stuff
And loads and loads of drills
I'm practising with both feet
Because one is not enough
Being a proper footballer is really, really tough

I know that I can do it
My dad is trying to help me
He's always on the sidelines
Trying hard not to shout

I want to be a footballer
And that's what I'm going to be
I'm not a silly daydreamer
Just you wait and see.

TJ Smith (8)
Springbank Academy, Eastwood

I Have A Secret Dragon

I have a secret dragon
Who is living in the tub
It greets me when I take a bath and
Gives my back a scrub
My parents cannot see it
They don't suspect it's there
And they look in all directions
And all they see is air
My dragon's very gentle
My dragon's very kind
No matter how I pull its tail
My dragon doesn't mind
We splash around together
And play at silly things
When I'm finished bathing
It dries me with its wings.

Lucas Fowers (8)
Springbank Academy, Eastwood

In The Rainforest

R ain pouring down to the ground
A s the monkeys swing from the trees
I n the rainforest it is alive
N ew trees growing as life is flowing
F rogs and jaguars live among us
O celot eyes reflecting in the night
R eforestation is what we need in the world as the Earth bleeds
E nergy running through the roots
S carlet macaws are colourful and bright
T he tired rainforest sleeps tonight.

Kai Hayes (9)
Springbank Academy, Eastwood

Monster

My monster has large, round eyes
He has sharp, pointed teeth
His mouth is dark and wide
He has slimy, scaly skin.

My monster has a pointy, blue nose
His arms are long and thin
His body is enormous.

My monster lives in a dark, gloomy cave
He eats slimy snails and slugs
He walks large thundering steps
He has a very scary voice.

Oscar Woodcock (9)
Springbank Academy, Eastwood

Imagination

Purple turtle with a spell on its shell
Flying in the crystal blue sky
Flew with no clue what to do
Imagination's life's creation
Whatever you imagine can come to life
Mystical unicorns eating popcorn
A dinosaur on the seashore in space
Sparkly stars in the dark
Hearing innocent little meows of a cute little kitten.

Layla Hicking (8)
Springbank Academy, Eastwood

Share Your Nightmare

In the shadows in the dead of night,
The nightmares start to win their fight,
I toss and turn to hide my face,
The shadows begin to take their place.

Every thought makes me shiver,
My hands and legs start to quiver,
I know these dreams are not real,
It's just the way they make me feel.

L Elizabeth North (8)
Springbank Academy, Eastwood

Ready For Summer

S uncream, sunglasses and hats at the ready
U nder the umbrella, catching some shade
M adly hot in the sand with my bucket and spade
M unching on ice cream, and sipping lemonade
E verybody around me surfing the waves
R eady for bed to rest my sweaty head.

Laila-Mai Catchpole (8)
Springbank Academy, Eastwood

Dancer

D ancing on the floor and my feet are sore
A way flies the girl with straight, blonde hair
N othing can stop us
C rawling on the floor we start to fly
E very step we take, we fly away
R eady to finish, we pack the stage ready for the next person to dance.

Lilly Daykin (9)
Springbank Academy, Eastwood

Once Upon A Footballer

F is for famous
O is for overtime
O is for offside
T is for talented
B is for baller
A is for awful
L is for the last kick
L is for last minute
E is for everlasting dream
R is for realistic.

Charlie Needham (9)
Springbank Academy, Eastwood

Money

Penny, penny, little and round
Special and shiny brown.
2p, 2p, also round
And always shiny up and down.
One pound, pound, a lot of money
You could spend this on some honey.
Five pounds, five pounds, it's special and blue
This is where you'll see the King too.

Maddie Watson (8)
Springbank Academy, Eastwood

All The Monsters

When I look under my bed, it's pitch-black
But when I look really close, I see dark green eyes
And I look again and see sharp white claws
The next day, I popped my head under
And I saw purple and sharp spikes and I looked again
And it made me scream, I saw a monster!

Emmie Belcher (9)
Springbank Academy, Eastwood

My Dreams Of A Racing Car

I love racing cars
My dream is to drive really fast
I want to buy a racing car
So I can go really fast
I love the noise as the racing car goes past
As I enter the pit my tyres need changing
Quickly, off I go.

James Vincett (9)
Springbank Academy, Eastwood

You Can Believe In A Dream

Everyone has a dream in mind
They think their dream can be real
Life can be different and hard
They struggle but believe in themselves
Hold onto your dream, it will become real.

Nathan Stanton-Meakin (8)
Springbank Academy, Eastwood

Tour Of The Universe

I drift off into a silent sleep.
I dream that I took a giant leap,
And I float and I fly,
Fly beyond the midnight sky.

Instead of seeing Venus, Jupiter and Mars,
I see something greater than the stars.
I see something unusual, different and new,
In all of these planets right in my view.

I gasped at a world made of nothing but books.
I laughed at a land where bunnies fly on rocks.
I gaped at a place where the men were as small as a fly.
Then the most spectacular planet caught my eye.

A planet, where funky blue plants jiggle and dance.
I started to groove too, wiggle and prance.
Alas, though I desperately wanted to stay,
I woke up in my bed and there I lay.

Isabel Potter (10)
St Thomas Of Canterbury Catholic Primary School, Mitcham

Once Upon A Dream

One wintry, inky night,
A couple of beautiful lit dots come to my sight.
What could these be?
Its light blinds, but somehow I can still see.
Tossing and turning in my bed,
I start to wonder, *isn't the light ruby-red?*
What could these be?
I ask myself again.
How many even are there? One... two... ten!
This feels like a dream...
I count again... What? Fifteen?!
More and more appear each second,
I've seen something no one has ever seen before!
I'm a legend!
I run up to the window and cry!
How glamorous is the night sky!
After a minute or two,
I start to think this is too good to be true!
But my happiness ends just a few seconds after,
Something happened! A disaster!
I was back in bed, staring at the early morning sky,
This had all been a lie.
Not a lie, a dream,

I wanted to scream!
But instead of a scream, I let out a smile,
I remembered that everything goes away after a while.

Gabriela Sacewicz (10)
St Thomas Of Canterbury Catholic Primary School, Mitcham

My Dream Record

I always have a dream record when I wake up,
I decide, was it jolly and fun, or dull and miserable,
But this one, I made all my friends pop up,
And I told them my dream and to me, everybody went invisible.

I enter a city by a door with number seventy-six,
With my best friend Gabriela, we started our journey there,
We could hear the horse's hooves click,
Suddenly, beside us, walking brave, was an army.

Soon after, a weird-looking man came up to us young ladies,
"You two, come with me," the man whispered creepily,
When we finally stopped he spoke,
"I am a part of Hades!"
Without warning, music started to play,
A song called *Melody!*

After a long time of silence, Gabriela asked,
"What year is it anyway?"
His face looked very confused like we weren't okay,
"It's 1891," the shade responded, looking at the lifeless day,

We went quiet for a bit, knowing we time-travelled
And then he gave us a spray.

"This grants you with powers," shade stated,
Me and Gabriela were very surprised at this discovery,
Without a sound, everything began to swirl,
And soon enough, I was back in reality, elated,
It felt so real, it took me an hour for recovery.

Julia Warian (10)
St Thomas Of Canterbury Catholic Primary School, Mitcham

Spinning Planets

Spinning planets in cosmic ballet,
Dance through the vastness,
Night and day.
Orbiting in celestial trance,
A cosmic waltz,
A mystic dance.
Mercury's whispers,
Swift and sly,
Venus adorned in evening sky.
Earth, a cradle of life so rare,
Breathes with rhythm,
A tender air.
Saturn dons rings, a jewelled crown,
Neptune's depths,
In oceanic gown.
Celestial symphony, a cosmic choir,
Spinning planets,
Sparks of celestial fire.

Georgette Nyamekeh (10)
St Thomas Of Canterbury Catholic Primary School, Mitcham

A Mysterious Shed

As I go ahead,
I see a mysterious shed,
I stepped in and saw a wizard,
Who led me with his pet lizard.

Two butterflies fly across the sky,
As the birds fly high,
The smell of limes,
Sifted through my nose,
As the koala does its pose.

The slithering snakes creep into the grass,
As the crocodiles are ready to chase,
The fishes swam through the pond
When I saw a magic wand.

Charlotte Nalukobe (11)
St Thomas Of Canterbury Catholic Primary School, Mitcham

Nightmares

N ever thought this would happen,
I was lost in the blackness,
G nome was staring at me,
H owever, I wasn't free,
T ime will tell,
M oments later, I fell,
"A re you okay?" I heard a voice say,
R esting in confusion,
E erie voices speaking,
S uddenly, I was back in bed.

Zuzanna Ogrodnik (11)
St Thomas Of Canterbury Catholic Primary School, Mitcham

Candy Land

C andy Land, what a wonderful place, different sweets everywhere.
A nybody can come here, doesn't matter about your skin or your race; nowhere else is like it, a fanfare of flames to try. Somewhere magical to be ensnared.
N owhere like it, infinite colours, infinite flavours clustered in Candy Land. Enter this magical world of sweets not withered by age.
D on't leave this place, so turn the next page for it is Candy Land, eat fantastical flying saucers, running Refreshers never changed by age.
Y ou will love it here, so step inside. Come on this fantastical ride to Candy Land.

L ollipops galore, go to Candy Lane with gingerbread houses and toxic waste rivers, it is a fabulous grandstand of sweets with sugary sand.
A stray you could be led but seventh star to the left and keep on going, you will find the fantastical fairyland, so come to Candyland.
N obody will know you've been gone, this flare has fizz galore, you will be in awe, so come to the fantastical fairyland.
D on't worry, we have a space for you, so come straight here. We'll see you tomorrow in Candy Land.

Kieran Quick (11)
Tockington Manor School, Tockington

Magic Dreams

M oving, creepiness suddenly bright, wanting to scream and shout out in fright.
A sudden urge, wanted me to see what it was.
G rabbing my dressing gown, I stumbled out of bed, trying to guess what was there.
I tiptoed to the door as quickly as possible. I was just about to open it when a noise blasted through my window.
C losing the window I saw a star shine really brightly in the sky. "Wow!" I exclaimed.

D ashing out of the door and streaking down the hallway to my front door felt thrilling.
R esisting before opening it, worrying what I might go through.
E ven though I was a little scared, I pushed open the door to reveal an...
A mazing swimming pool. I love swimming and I am going to use it every day.
M aking my way back to my bed was crazy.
S uddenly I heard my dad's voice saying it was time for school. Maybe it was a dream after all.

Sienna Ricciardi (10)
Tockington Manor School, Tockington

Candy Land

Every night I can't wait to go to bed,
And see all the wonderful dreams from inside my head.
Tonight I want to go to Candy Land,
With giant gingerbread houses that are simply grand!
Luxury hot chocolate lakes and isomalt bridges,
Marshmallow mountains and sugar-loving witches.
I imagine myself soaring through the sky,
Looking down from way up high.
Eating buffets of candyfloss clouds,
Flying so gracefully that I attract crowds!
I spot someone waving from the lollipop lagoon,
So I float down on a popcorn balloon.
I say hi to the mermaid waving at me,
She tells me it's time to go back home.
"No!" I plead,
"Yes," she says, "You can come again."
I guess I'll see Candy Land next time I sleep,
I whisper to myself as I close my eyes and pull up my sheets.

Nitsa Bhadri (11)
Tockington Manor School, Tockington

Back Into The Past

There were two footballers
They met a T-rex and three other people
So myself and Jordan Pickford challenged them to a football match
So we played
Pickford played number one for us
And I played number nine
The other team was Emma's
She played in the number one position
Connie played number two
Siri was number six
And T-rex played opposite me as number nine
So we played...
My terrific team scored
In the first two minutes... such excitement
Scored by Preece one-nil
Then the dinosaurs scored
T-rex scored
So the score is one-one... all to play for
Everyone trying their best
Hot and sweaty
It was full-time... Ref blew hard on the whistle
And then it went to penalties

The pressure, the anticipation...
Who would win?
Which team would triumph?
In the end, the best team won - us!

Harry Preece (10)
Tockington Manor School, Tockington

Dream On

Dream on like you have never dreamt before,
I clambered on the bed with the teddy bear I bore,
As I gently closed my drowsy eyes,
I soon became part of an enchanted disguise.

Poof! Beside me, a live teddy bear appeared,
It swam in the air and its eyes peered,
As I stroked this furry divine,
In a flash, I suddenly realised that the bear was mine.

In the blink of an eye, I was floating,
It felt like we went out boating,
We sat at the cave's mouth, talking,
While the stars looked like they were walking.

Suddenly, I saw my little sis shaking me awake,
Telling me that I had to eat some cake,
As I started to clamber off the bed with the teddy bear I bore,
I thought to myself, *dream like you have never dreamt before.*

Sirivaana Vankdoth (10)
Tockington Manor School, Tockington

Magic Mysteries

M oving, mystic, a small, sharp movement around,
A utumn is nearing, leaves on the ground, no flowers yet found,
G rabbing my dressing gown, tying it as I go,
I n midnight I walk through the snow,
C reeping around through the dark, wondering what's there,

M ay I be dreaming? Is this all true?
Y ears feel like they've gone by,
S tars in the sky, oh! A shooting star!
T ell me, shall I make a wish?
E very day I wish I could fly,
R ight up through the sky,
I wonder why late at night, you have a dream, it's just your mind processing the day,
E veryone, night-night.
S ilence.

Isabel Pickavance (11)
Tockington Manor School, Tockington

This Poem Isn't Meant To Rhyme

This poem isn't meant to rhyme,
Hang on a minute, what's the time?
Oh dear, this isn't going well,
Look, that dragon's flying well!
I guess I'll have to start again,
I'll add some hope and joy but then,
I forgot to say,
By the way,
This poem isn't meant to rhyme,
I just had dreamed that it'd be fine,
I feel like I need to start again,
But then,
Look, a unicorn,
It's rather sparkly,
Yes,
I'm doing it!
The fairies are twinkly,
Closing my eyes,
It's like a dream!
I will not let my poem rhyme and...
There goes the alarm,

Sitting up, I rub my eyes,
Hello, sun, it's waking time!

Amal Lachab (10)
Tockington Manor School, Tockington

Dreams

In my dream, I dream...
of being a gymnast with a crowd cheering me on.
When the bright lights shine in my eyes,
I leap into the air and jump into an aerial.
When I come to a landing, I visualise a perfect ten.
As my performance comes to an end,
the judges pull me aside and ask me if I would like to join the best gymnastics academy in England.
I am so excited that I ask all my friends to come for a sleepover!
They all accept my invite, but I don't see them anywhere.
I still keep looking, but I can't see anyone there.
As I was about to leave, they surprised me with the party.

Avneet Chohan (11)
Tockington Manor School, Tockington

Alien Planet

Tonight, I'm going to my special place with the aliens in outer space,
Alien planet is the place I go to in my dreams,
I'm not like those kids who dream of floating in cookies and cream,
In my sleep, I go wherever I want to be,
I want to be in my spaceship, flying,
From my spaceship, I see Alien Planet,
On the planet I see this alien holding this sort of gadget,
It's filming me with a camera,
I'm the first human they've seen on Alien Planet.
Weird things happen on Alien Planet.
Tonight I'm in my special place,
With the aliens in outer space.

Ruby Layade (11)
Tockington Manor School, Tockington

Untitled

I close my eyes,
Turn out the lights,
And wish for my thoughts to be wise.
Through the night struggling,
Sometimes shivering.
By the time midnight arrives,
Soon I fall asleep.
I never dream,
Space in and out,
Floating in blackness alone.
Then in the morn,
Being sucked out of the darkness,
I see blinding lights,
Then a dark shadow.
Looking at my clock, reminding me of reality,
Stretching and yawning, rising from my bed,
Hearing a voice quite high, then seeing my brother.
It gives me a smile on my face.

George Griffith (10)
Tockington Manor School, Tockington

A Wonderful Dream

Dreams are like stars in the moonlight sky
Shimmering, shining
Like leaves on a cherry blossom tree
Dancing beautifully in the wind
The grass prancing around
The wind-like waves over colourful flowers
Dreams are friends and some enemies
At the end of the day, a dream's a dream
But it's a new adventure every time
So have a happy time in your dream
Because they only happen once.

Albie Palmer (10)
Tockington Manor School, Tockington

Woods Wonderland Dream

In the woods, enchanted mist I see,
The opposite of cotton candy tea,
In the dark with unimaginable animals,
Hearing random whistles,
I can sense something weird coming,
Kapow! What is it...
OMG, I kinda know what it is,
It's a-a-a half-unicorn, half-monkey
It's my dream animal...
I can't believe what I see,
Oh, morning,
Hang on, it was a dream.

Emma Fudulu (10)
Tockington Manor School, Tockington

Dreams

D ragons are flying above me in my dreams.
R ace cars are going as fast as possible in my dreams.
E veryone is happy and they can do what they want in my dreams.
A mazing people like Harry Potter are in my dreams.
M agical powers and flying are in my dreams.
S trange things happen, like flying people in my dreams.

Stanley Baigent (11)
Tockington Manor School, Tockington

The Brilliant Ben Stokes

The bat swings as fast as light,
Hit it out the ground,
Out of the pitch into the crowd,
He's bowling the ball as fast as lightening,
Making the stumps go flying.
On the boundary jump high, there he is,
Catching him just as quick as a flying bird,
There it is the match is over,
What a performance from the one and only Ben Stokes.

Maximilian Hunt (11)
Tockington Manor School, Tockington

Darkness

D arkness closing in on all sides
A ll hope is lost
R estlessness won't get you anywhere
K een to get back to reality
N ot a chance to escape
E xcept a small crack in the wall
S ounds to me like a way out
S uddenly I'm surrounded by colours, it was just a dream.

Leon Francken (10)
Tockington Manor School, Tockington

Dragon Fire

Fire, fire, burning bright,
Through the darkness of the night,
Soaring high up in the sky,
Dragon fire lights up the sky.

Burning bright, burning strong,
Dragon fire, it belongs,
Dragon fire, flying high,
Lighting up the moonlit sky,
Dark and dangerous, burning bright,
Lighting up the moonlit night.

Oliver Galpin (10)
Tockington Manor School, Tockington

I Had A Dream

I had a dream
I was in Candy Land
It was grand
I had a gingerbread house
There was even a chocolate mouse
And there were candyfloss clouds
It wasn't too loud
The rainbow was made out of sweets
There were so many treats
But I guess it was all just a dream.

Emma Strickland (10)
Tockington Manor School, Tockington

Angel

A dramatic land of fluffy clouds levitates above me
N othing can stop me from being free
G lowing, bright yellow beams of magic
E nding could be so tragic
L osing all signs of hope, the sunrise will energise the angel's life.

Sophia Heer (11)
Tockington Manor School, Tockington

Rugby

R ough sport with lots of hard, pushing contact.
U nder lots of pressure when the game makes such an impact.
G iving 100% each time you play.
B attered legs and arms every single day.
Y ou may get lucky and win the game!

Joseph Leadbeater (11)
Tockington Manor School, Tockington

Danger

Exploring planets is what I love,
I'm an astronaut flying up above,
A new planet! Let's explore,
Me and my best friend, Diney the dinosaur,
We are excited, what will we find?
I can see castles, unicorns and clouds in my mind,
As we get closer, it becomes clear,
This planet is something to fear,
It's dark, ghostly and freezing cold,
Me and Diney were told, "You must be bold."
We were just about to land on this planet that looked scary,
When out of the dark comes a creature, big and hairy,
We didn't fancy our chances,
So we landed and ran without any backward glances,
We didn't think it would get any more frightening,
But then, a massive bolt of lightening,
Diney started to cry, he got such a fright,
I hugged him tight and told him, "We have to fight."
But the monster was back and I began to scream,
And just at that point, I woke up from my dream,
What a relief, thank goodness for that I thought,
Sometimes it's hard being an astronaut.

Rhea Mclean (9)
Wistow Parochial CofE (VC) School, Wistow

In My Dreams

Once upon a dream,
I wanted to ride a submarine,
Or be a bus driver,
Even a skydiver.

I wish I could live in my dreams,
I hope it's as it seems,
I could be a footballer,
I would need to grow taller.

I could be a movie star,
Maybe even a person who fixes cars,
So many things I could be,
I might be a cook and cook tea.

Loads to choose,
What if I could be a detective and find clues?
They're just my dreams,
I'll just wait till I'm in my teens.

Isabella Haddon (10)
Wistow Parochial CofE (VC) School, Wistow

My Brain Is A Dream Factory

As I snuggle close,
In my warm and comfy bed,
I start to drift off,
And I start to dream instead.

I love my dreams,
I can dream of anything at all,
I can escape the daytime humdrum,
When I answer, my dreamtime calls.

Sometimes dreams are happy,
I awake feeling rested,
But when those dreams are bad,
My mood is really tested.

I liked the dream where I could fly,
I was magic and had superpowers,
I rescued dogs from bogs,
I was the hero of the hour.

Annabelle Davis (9)
Wistow Parochial CofE (VC) School, Wistow

Once Upon A Star

Once upon a star
On green grass
With clouds as warm
There was a dream.

With stars in the sky
The sky purple like grapes
The smell of roses red
And the feel of a cosy, warm bed.

Dreams about pirates
Dreams about dragons
Dreams about knights
And meteorites.

A brave knight he is
With grey, shiny armour
And his name is Kaydon
Who needs to save a maiden.

What will happen in the vision?
Will he conquer his mission?

Scarlett Wilson (8)
Wistow Parochial CofE (VC) School, Wistow

Sailing With The Stars

I have a dream every night
Where stars are gazing at me, oh-so-bright
I am lying on my boat, drifting out to sea
And I feel like the stars are protecting me
The invisible shield cast around me
Makes me feel so calm and happy
The stars around me get nearer and nearer
And the dream gets clearer and clearer
The stars came down and lifted my book
I went up and up until I could float
Up to the heavens where dreams come true
Dancing with the stars, me and you.

Lorna Wood (9)
Wistow Parochial CofE (VC) School, Wistow

Henry The Wizard

Once, a little boy wanted to be a wizard,
So he practised and practised and ended up
with a lizard.
He magicked a rabbit right out of his hat,
And turned his big brother into a rat.
He wanted to use his wizardry wand for good,
But nothing went exactly as it should.
He moved his wand with energy and delight,
But all he got was a frightful sight.
One day, his mum said, "You don't need a wand,
It's in you, forever and beyond."

Georgia Pavey (8)
Wistow Parochial CofE (VC) School, Wistow

Spiders Crawling

Spiders crawling,
While I'm drawing,
My family can see,
There is so much glee.

Different kinds,
Climb up me from behind,
Their webs are falling,
Falling and crawling.

My family run away,
Although they did not betray,
My trust is still unbroken,
And none of them have spoken...

Suddenly they flee,
My family can see,
There is so much sadness,
But my family were full of gladness.

Lydia Jones (10)
Wistow Parochial CofE (VC) School, Wistow

Dreams Can Be Anything

D inosaurs, dinosaurs, roaming the land
R elaxed people, holding hands
E xotic creatures, flying around
A mazed children in the playground
M agical fairies casting spells
S uper elves climbing the fells.

Florence Ibson (10)
Wistow Parochial CofE (VC) School, Wistow

My Fog

Once upon a time,
I was in a line,
And a little girl lay in the sky,
But a little green frog skipped by,
And had glared her in the eye,
She had never noticed,
But she did find a little lotus.

Luisa Kehoe (9)
Wistow Parochial CofE (VC) School, Wistow

YOUNG WRITERS INFORMATION

We hope you have enjoyed reading this book – and that you will continue to in the coming years.

If you're a young writer who enjoys reading and creative writing, or the parent of an enthusiastic poet or story writer, do visit our website **www.youngwriters.co.uk**. Here you will find free competitions, workshops and games, as well as recommended reads, a poetry glossary and our blog.

If you would like to order further copies of this book, or any of our other titles, then please give us a call or visit **www.youngwriters.co.uk**.

Young Writers
Remus House
Coltsfoot Drive
Peterborough
PE2 9BF
(01733) 890066
info@youngwriters.co.uk

- **YoungWritersUK**
- **YoungWritersCW**
- **youngwriterscw**
- **youngwriterscw**